THE DEADLY REGATTA

Abigail Summers Cozy Mysteries
Book 3

ANN PARKER

Copyright © 2024 by Ann Parker

Layout design and Copyright © 2024 by Next Chapter

Published 2024 by Next Chapter

Cover art by Lordan June Pinote

This book is a work of fiction. Names, characters, places, and incidents are the product of the author's imagination or are used fictitiously. Any resemblance to actual events, locales, or persons, living or dead, is purely coincidental.

All rights reserved. No part of this book may be reproduced or transmitted in any form or by any means, electronic or mechanical, including photocopying, recording, or by any information storage and retrieval system, without the author's permission.

Dedicated to all my grandchildren - Reece, Lewis, Harvey, Layla, Holly, Isla, Isabella and Liliana.

And thank you to psychic medium, Tania Angel, for being the inspiration for Hayley Moon.

Also by Ann Parker

The Deadly Detective Agency

The Deadly Pub Quiz

Ottersmill Marina is located on the picturesque River Gore and nestles at the foot of the Chiltern Hills. It boasts a licensed sailing club, a chandlery and moorings for fifty boats. Our Regatta weekend is held every August. We apologise for the horrific murder at this year's event and hope it didn't spoil your enjoyment of the occasion.

Chapter 1

LITTLE JACOB REDMAN WAS SIX YEARS OLD AND HE was bored and hot. Daddy had told him that this geratta was going to be fun. Well, it wasn't. He couldn't even see the races, not even a boat. All he could see were bottoms and legs. There were some people who had seats at the start and finish line, but not them. Just the posh ones, Daddy said. But they were posh, weren't they? Daddy had his own window cleaning business. It wasn't fair that his brother, Josh, was allowed to stand at the water's edge with all his friends. And he was taking part in the raft race later on. He was never coming to the Ottersmill Geratta ever again. There weren't even any otters.

"Can we go now, Dad?" Jacob asked, while pulling on his dad's shorts.

"Not yet. The races are still going on."

"I'm hungry."

"You're always hungry and we've already eaten. I'm not paying any more of those prices. You can wait till we get home."

"Can I sit on your shoulders then?"

"It's too hot for that, Jacob. It won't be long now."

But he'd said that ages ago. This was even more boring than

going shopping with Mummy when she needed a dress for Auntie Dawn's wedding. When she bought him clothes, she just held them against him, but no, she had to try on everything in hundreds of shops. Even if he could see the boats, he wasn't interested. He liked coming to the river to feed the ducks and the swans, but there weren't any to be seen today. It was far too noisy. Every time the horns went or the gun started a race, the cheers and shouts would start. Maybe they were up on the bend, where it was quiet.

Jacob had enjoyed it when they visited all the marquees, which were covered in colourful bunting and flags. And Mum had let him have a big ice cream after the burger from the truck. But even Mummy and Daddy were straining to see the racing boats. Even the boats were boring. He liked the ones with the big white sales that went zigzagging up the river. After the third time of being told they couldn't leave, Jacob decided on a plan.

Mummy and Daddy wouldn't even notice if he crept quietly away. It would be worth getting in trouble to go and see the swans. He wouldn't go near the edge; that always made Mummy angry. If only he had saved a bit of his bread roll for them.

He made sure his parents weren't looking and then weaved his way through the dense crowd, none of whom took any notice of the small child, dressed in a dinosaur T-shirt and green shorts. He glanced behind him and was relieved that he had left them all behind and no one was coming after him. He might even get away with it if he didn't stay too long, so he started to run. Jacob rounded the bend in the river and saw the weeping willow tree where the ducks and swans were usually found. There was a small pontoon, with mooring for one boat, but as the tree was so overgrown it was seldom used. He bent down to get under the branches because he had seen something glinting. The ducks weren't there, but all four swans were, and they swam expectantly towards the boy for their usual treats, but they were to be disappointed. Jacob knew he shouldn't have, but he went closer to the edge. It was then that he noticed a patch of red on the usually white feathers, and for the first time that day, he actually saw something in the river.

Mrs Redman joined in the clapping when she heard that a team from Ottersmill had won the women's scull race. She looked down to speak to Jacob and her heart skipped a beat when her youngest child wasn't there.

"Jacob," she called. First gently and then loudly as panic set in. Mr Redman shouted for his son too, and pushed the other spectators out of the way as he made his way towards the front, by the riverbank. Maybe he had gone to see his brother, but Josh said he hadn't seen him, but wondered if he had gone to see the ducks by the big willow, as he had mentioned them at least twenty times that day. His mum also remembered he had kept asking where the otters were, so she hoped and prayed that he had gone to the place upstream that he knew. They rushed as fast as all the people would let them pass, and it was as they got nearer that they heard the screaming.

Chapter 2

PC TOM BENNETT AND WPC JANE NICHOLS WERE trying their best to keep the spectators of the Ottersmill Regatta back. However, it seemed everyone was much too interested in the dead body that was lying on a rubber sheet by the riverbank. They had put up the crime scene tape and were waiting for the arrival of Tom's nemesis, Detective Chief Inspector Tony Johnson.

The forensic team, in their white overalls, began erecting the white, pop-up tent to put over the cold, wet corpse of Leo Spencer, who had been pulled out of the River Gore. His glazed blue eyes were open and he looked as shocked as everyone else that someone had murdered him. He had been identified by many of the bystanders as the commodore of the sailing club. Even in death, he still looked smart in his blazer, grey flannel trousers and yellow and blue tie in the colours of the club pennant.

Tom hoped the Chief Constable would send any detective other than Johnson to investigate this one, knowing that he would hate all the boating community, as he did anyone who flaunted their wealth. Mind you, thought Tom, he didn't like the hoi polloi much either. He showed the same respect to a Lord as he did a labourer. In fact, even less. But Johnson saved his real contempt for the young constable himself, because he was always one step in front of him and managed to get to the truth of cases before he did. Johnson had an idea how, but couldn't say for sure. He would be the one who was laughed at if he said he thought it was Hayley, Bennett's psychic wife, who was feeding him information. He couldn't prove it yet, but he would one day.

Tom thought his boss would have gone mad if he knew that as soon as he and Jane had arrived there, he had phoned Hayley and told her there had been a suspicious death, likely murder, at the Ottersmill Regatta. She had been a perfectly normal, but slightly eccentric wife, until the day a spirit named Abigail Summers had burst into their home, wanting to know who had murdered her. Knowing her as he did now, he was surprised the list hadn't been a lot longer. But with his help as well, Abigail had worked out who did it and decided to open The Deadly Detective Agency. Several other spirits made up the team, but Hayley was the link between the living and the dead. Unfortunately, he was the link between them and the police. The Chief Constable suspected, and was happy about that, but Johnson did everything he could to get rid of him, and he had to watch his back constantly. Especially when he needed to get copies of post-mortems or interviews for the others. Talk of the devil, thought Tom, as the two young constables heard shouting. Yep, the boss had arrived.

DCI Johnson, followed by his sergeant, Dave Mills, pushed his way through the crowd. The two policemen couldn't be more different. Johnson always looked like he had just got out of bed and forgotten to brush his hair, but Mills on the other hand had an immaculate haircut and always wore a fitted suit and crisp shirt.

"Don't stand there doing nothing, Bennett, get this lot out of the way. First, tell me who's died and ruined my Sunday," yelled Johnson.

"The club's commodore, Leo Spencer, sir." Tom pointed to a family standing to his left. The father was wrapped in a blanket and the mother was bending down and hugging her smallest child. "The young son, Jacob Redman, went missing and saw the body floating in the water at about half past three. The father arrived soon after and jumped straight in, then shouted for help and a couple of men managed to get the body on the bank. One of them tried to resuscitate him, but it was too late. It was then that they noticed the big gash on the side of his head."

"He could have fallen in and bashed his head on that staging. Or been hit by a boat or an oar. I might be able to get back to my pint then."

"The boats didn't come up this far, they went downstream from the start line at the Ottersmill Sailing Club, towards the Jolly Sailor at Tingleford. The other way goes towards Gorebridge. As you see, the bend in the river hides this area from the view of everyone, so no one has come forward to say they saw anything so far. And this is the widest part of the river, so no one on the opposite bank will have been able to see much. Also, sir, the same little boy saw this on the bank under the tree when he saw the body. It was hidden under the boughs of the willow." Tom pointed to a large steel bar that had been put in a bag and had a dark stain on one of the pointed edges. "They could have both been hidden for weeks if the boy hadn't gone on a duck hunt."

"Remind me to thank him," Johnson answered sarcastically. "Is the next of kin here?"

"There is a Mrs Ruth Spencer, but we haven't been able to find her yet. She was here apparently, but seems to have disappeared."

"It's always the spouse. Isn't that right, Sergeant?"

Mills thought that in his experience it very rarely was, but didn't want to annoy the boss this early on, so he just agreed with him, but added, "Have an ask around, Tom, and see if you can find anyone that has got her phone number. She might be in one of the tents or somewhere. It's strange she hasn't heard about it, unless she's gone home."

"Righto, sir." Tom was delighted that he would have the chance to leave the crime scene and do some digging of his own. Jane Nichols rolled her eyes as she was left to do crowd control on her own, but more that she was left to work with Johnson. He wasn't too keen on women either, so Tom definitely owed her one.

Mills got his notebook out and walked over to have a word with the Redmans. The poor man had been in the water and needed to get home. He addressed the young lad first. "Hello. My name is Sergeant Mills. How are you feeling, Jacob?"

"It wasn't me. He was in the water when I got here."

The older child, Josh, was happy to answer. "He was dead, with all this blood pouring everywhere, and you could see his brains coming out through a big hole in his head. And his huge, scary eyes were staring at us."

"Don't exaggerate, Josh," said his mother. "Take no notice. He's just thinking of what he can tell his friends at school when he goes back."

"How old is he, Mrs Redman?"

"Nine and Jacob is six. Is it right it was the commodore?"

"That's what we think so far. He'll have to be officially identified. Did you see anyone else when you came up here, Jacob? Or walking away, or going up the towpath?" A shake of the head was all he got in return. "Perhaps you could ask him later for me, Mrs Redman. He might remember more when he's got over the shock." Mills asked her husband "Did any of you know the deceased? Have you got a boat here?"

"We wish. No, I'm just a humble window cleaner. 'Redman's

Windows & Gutters', if you ever need one. We are local so we come to the regatta when we get the chance."

"I'm sorry to ask, but because you found the body, could you tell me where you were earlier, please? I daresay you can alibi each other, so it's just a formality."

"Of course, we've been together all day. Mainly watching the races or having something to eat."

Josh put his hand up excitedly. "Apart from when Dad went to the beer tent and the toilet. He was gone ages. Even Mum said she couldn't think where he'd got to. Remember, Mum?"

"Thank you, Josh," said his father quickly. "I'd forgotten about that. But I'm sure there are a lot of people who saw me. And there was a long queue for the portaloos. That was why I was so long." He ruffled his son's hair but looked more like he wanted to give him a clip round the ear, Mills thought.

He took their phone number and address and said they could go. Although someone would need to speak to them again, he told them. As he walked back to the scene of the crime, he smiled to himself as he heard Jacob say, "Can we feed the swans now, Mummy?" Not too shocked then. He got a swift reply from his mother as she gave him a stern lecture on why he was never allowed to go anywhere ever again for running off and scaring the life out of her.

DCI Johnson saw someone in the crowd taking photos with a large camera. He recognised him from press conferences in the past. Bloody journos, he thought. "Use it and lose it, mate."

"Detective Chief Inspector, I'm just covering the regatta for the Chiltern Weekly."

"I don't see no boats. Get lost, son."

"Don't be like that, Tony. Murder or accident?"

"I'll give an update in the morning after we've found out for ourselves. But put it this way, I don't think Sergeant Mills here will be getting back home to give his baby a bath tonight. Bennett, what are you still doing here? Get going and find the wife. And if anyone asks, the regatta is now over, but no one can leave yet. I'll get some more uniforms over here to take names. But I'll need a list of all the boat owners and committee members."

"Sir," said Tom happily. "I'll get right on it." Some proper police work at last. And he'd better keep an eye out for Hayley and warn her that DCI Johnson was in his usual foul mood, as she should be arriving any minute now.

Chapter 3

AT THAT SAME MOMENT, PC TOM'S WIFE, HAYLEY Bennett, the psychic medium, was driving rather too fast down the lanes from Ridgeway Woods, where she had been having a Sunday stroll with the three spirits, Abigail, Terry, and Betty. They were all the founder members of The Deadly Detective Agency and had raced to the car when they received the call from Tom, saying that there had been a murder at the regatta. Hayley was convinced she was lost, but then she had to turn on two wheels when she saw a small board with an arrow that led the way to Ottersmill Marina.

There was nowhere to park, not even a space for her tiny red Mini, so she reversed back until she found a place. It didn't help that two marked police cars were blocking the entrance.

"Now guys, before we get there, please don't make me look like an idiot. Try to remember that I'm the only one that can see you, so don't make me talk to myself. When I answer you, give me a chance to get my phone out, so it looks like I'm not crazy."

"Whatever you say, Hayley," said Terry and Betty. Abigail swore on her life, which didn't really give Hayley a lot of hope.

Abigail added, "It's a shame Lillian isn't here. She's so good with the dead bodies." Lillian Yin was a nurse when she was alive and had a way of getting to the cause and even the time of death straight away. "But I still think that should be our first port of call. Get it, boats. No? We'll have a look at the victim and then try to find out from Tom what's going on."

"You mean I will, hun. Hopefully, they have another detective in charge, but I bet Johnson's there. I have a premonition."

"Me too, and I'm not psychic," said Betty sadly. Betty was a sprightly eighty-two-year-old who had been married to John for over sixty years. She had died a week after him, so was enjoying some 'me time'. Not to mention every murder that they investigated was a highlight to the wannabe sleuth.

"Going by the crowd, I'd say we'll find the body over there," said Terry. He had been the leader of the Deads who all met in the Becklesfield Public Library. That was until Abigail Summers had stumbled into their deaths and taken over. But he was getting used to this bossy, but brilliant woman. The two of them had even been on a couple of dates, admittedly one of them had ended in a murder, but when did true love ever run smooth?

He led the way, and when he realised that Abigail wasn't barking her usual orders, he turned around to see why. He shook his head as he saw the three women were staring at two rowers in tight lycra shorts. Terry noticed the one with the tanned legs and bulging muscles was bending over getting his oars out. Hayley lifted her sunglasses on the top of her long black hair to get a better look.

"Get a move on, you lot. We've got a murder to solve," he shouted.

"Yes," said Abigail. "Let's go. We've got to get to the bottom of him. I mean the bottom of it," she giggled while not moving.

"That reminds me, hun, I've got to pick up two buns on the way home," said Hayley laughing. She'd already forgotten that she was standing on her own and an elderly man gave her a puzzled look. Hayley went bright red and just hoped he hadn't heard what she had said.

"Oh my," said Betty, "I'm sorry, Terry dear, but he has got the full monty, hasn't he?" she added. Terry felt even more envious to see he was just as good-looking from the front, with his dark wavy hair and wrap-around sports sunglasses.

"I know what Abigail is like, but I'm surprised at you, Betty."

"You know what they say, Terry, there's many who can fiddle with an old tune, or something like that. You know what I mean. My strings are just a bit looser these days, that's all." Betty had a wealth of sayings and seldom got them right or in the correct order. But that was part of her charm.

Abigail said, "You know my methods, Terry, I like to look at things from all angles, inch by inch. And who knows, he might be a sus sex. I mean suspect."

"Well, I volunteer to stake him out if you know what I mean," laughed Betty. "Keep him under surveillance."

Terry shook his head again. Women didn't behave like that when he was alive fifty years ago. Men did the wolf-whistling then and made the comments. Girls in his day didn't even say the word sex. Let alone do it. Yep, there was no doubt about it; he was born about ninety years too soon, he thought wistfully. Not only that, he was a bit jealous that Abigail was staring like a love-struck teenager. "Er, dead person, remember?" he added impatiently.

They reluctantly averted their eyes and walked towards a white tent that had become visible over the heads of the onlookers. Terry and Betty noticed a young family standing some way from the others. Abigail only had eyes for the corpse, so she went straight to the tent.

Hayley gave a wave to her friend, Dave Mills, but she held her finger over her lips and nodded towards Johnson. He knew straight away what she meant. He had a feeling she was the reason that young Tom had a lot of good ideas on how to solve their murder cases. And if he had to get to the top on his coat-tails, then so be it. Hayley hid behind a large lady with a huge straw hat. But then she jumped out of her skin when she was tapped on her shoulder and dragged away.

"I thought you might turn up, Hayley. Well, I was hoping, if I'm honest."

"Lady Caroline. You took ten years off my life."

"Sorry, but I didn't want that awful Johnson to see me. You know I love to help you and Abigail." Lady Caroline Hatton was only one of a few people, apart from her policeman husband, that knew Hayley Moon - her professional name as a psychic medium - had help from the other side with the murders. They had met when Abigail was trying to solve her own murder, and one of the clues led them to the May Day Fayre at Chiltern Hall, where the Hattons lived. Even on a hot and humid day, Caroline looked cool and elegant in a cream linen trouser suit, with matching court shoes. Hayley always admired her style rather than her own hippy one. Whenever she wore linen, she ended up looking like a crumpled potato sack. And she could forget about heels these days. She tottered around like a drunk teenager, who had found a stash of cider.

"Tom called me as soon as the body was found, Caroline. He hates me interfering, but loves it when we help really. I'm sure he just makes out he doesn't. What are you doing here? I know you don't like boats."

"Somehow I was talked into presenting the prizes today. I'll have to find out if they are still going ahead with the rest of the programme. Such a shame for everyone. I gave some trophies to the young sailing cadets this morning and now I've got to give the Hatton Challenge Cup for the men's coxless doubles this afternoon." To anyone else, Hayley would have said I've just seen a pair that definitely weren't coxless, but decided against it. She was an aristocrat, after all. Caroline was saying, "Local actress Kirsty Peacock gave them out yesterday. But I do know a lot of the people involved, if that helps. I heard the victim is the present commodore, Leo Spencer. I don't know him to talk to, but I know his wife, Ruth, quite well. I haven't seen her and it's a wonder she hasn't heard about it by now. She's involved with the gymkhana that they want me to host at the Hall. She actually owns Cranston Stables if you've heard of it. It's about a mile from Becklesfield."

"Interesting. That is very useful to know. Abigail is looking at the body as we speak with Terry and Betty. I'm going to arrange a meeting at my house for tomorrow morning, at about ten, so we can say what we've all learned. Why don't you come, Caroline? You'll know much more than we do, I reckon. They'd all love to see you. It's 13, Church Lane, Becklesfield."

"I will, thank you. It's just a shame I can't see them!"

Over at the crime scene, Abigail was momentarily blinded by the flash of the cameras from the forensic team. She stood back against the side of the tent just in case they picked her up. In a past investigation, Tom had said there was some trouble with a few of the crime scene photos, as there were some suspicious lights and shadows obscuring the details. As soon as they had gone, though, she got to work. Whoever this smartly dressed man was, he was lying on a sheet and looked to be soaking wet. There was a dark red mark, if not a hole, on the side of his right temple. Even Lillian wouldn't have been able to tell if he had died immediately, as any blood that may have continued to bleed if he hadn't, would have been washed away by the current in the river. Abigail guessed him to be like her, in his late thirties, and going by his blazer, to be an important member of the club. Was that what had got him killed? It was sure going to be a tough one. With their past murders, there were at most ten suspects, but this one happened at the most important regatta in the county, so there were maybe hundreds of suspects. Oh well, she had faith in all the team. Apart from Johnson, of course. There must have been some truth to the devil saying that day, as the inspector and another man walked in at that very minute.

"So, Doctor, what have we got? Say an accident and I can get back to the Red Lion."

"You know the drill, Tony. Post-mortem first. I'll know more when I get him on the table, but I reckon our friend here was attacked face on by a left-handed killer and pushed in the water, where he drowned. But don't quote me yet. Once I've checked the lungs for water, I can tell you if he died instantly or not. That looks like the right weapon for the wound but it will have to be confirmed."

"Murder then. Bugger. I had a feeling I wasn't going to be that lucky. What does the weapon look like to you?"

The doctor had gloves on and it was in an evidence bag, so he picked it up. "I've got a boat here myself, when I get the damn chance to use it. Sometimes, I think I'm just paying the mooring fees for nothing. You know what they say—a boat is a hole in the water you throw money into. So I do happen to know what this is. This, Inspector, is a steel mooring spike or pin. If you're going down the river and want to moor, you just bash one of these on the bank and put the rope through this bit and tie it off. Most boats carry them."

"Hmm. Let's hope there are some prints then. So you're thinking it's someone that knew him from the club then and owned a boat?"

"Unless it just happened to be lying on the towpath. They're easy to leave behind when you undo the rope and motor off. But thankfully that's your job to work out, not mine."

Johnson put his hands in the pockets of his shiny grey suit.

"So premeditated, or they saw red and hit him. Okay, thanks, Doc. MILLS! Get in here. It's unofficially murder, so get the ball rolling. I'll ring the Chief Constable and tell him the bad news. Then I'll make my way to the club. I wonder what beer they have."

As soon as the detective and the doctor had gone, Abigail joined Terry and Betty and they walked to the point where the victim had fallen in the water and had a look around. Then they found Hayley to relay what they had learned about the body.

"I'm not an expert like Lillian," Abigail said and turned around to look at Terry, who thought that was funny, as she usually thought she was. "Thank you, Terry. But, looking at the injury and the depth of the wound, I'd say he must have been knocked out straight away, if not killed instantly. And, I would say he was hit by a left-handed murderer."

"Or a right-handed one from behind," challenged Terry.

"There was blood splatter by the river's edge, so he or she would have had to be walking on water. Yes, like me, Terry. No, he was facing his killer. We need to find out if he was meeting someone. It was odd that he went off in the middle of the races, on one of the most important days for the club."

Betty agreed. "It had to be something or someone very important. Maybe a woman."

"Lady Caroline told me that he's married to Ruth. She owns Cranston Stables. But that doesn't mean he wasn't meeting a girlfriend. I'm sure a commodore has more than a few admirers," said Hayley. Luckily she remembered to pretend to speak on her phone.

"With great power, comes great... I can't remember, actually."

"I think it's responsibility, Betty. But I think it comes with quite a few perks as well. Especially if you are as good looking as him. A young, rich, fancy dresser and he owns a boat. He probably had to fight them off," said Abigail. "Not that he's my type of course, Terry."

"Ah, so you're saying I'm not young, good looking, or a fancy dresser," said Terry.

"Well, you're good looking," laughed Abigail. "Ooh, he's not here is he?" Terry was always the first to see the Deads, as he called them.

"No, thank Heavens. He must have passed straight on. They usually do. It's when they don't realise that they are dead that they hang around."

"Shame," said Abigail and Betty at the same time. "I just mean that we could have asked who hit him," Abigail added.

"Sure you did," replied Terry with a smile that he reserved only for her. He was very handsome in a rugged way. He was in his fifties when he died, in the nineteen eighties and he loved all his friends at the library. They had become his family that he never had in life. It was only since Abigail herself had died that she had helped him find his real family. They had been on a job in an old farming cottage in Windmill Lane, and he could describe the fireplace and the house before he went in. He had been brought up in an orphanage and had never felt he had belonged. But with the help of Hayley, Abigail, and the village parish records, he had found out that he had lived there before he was five. It was then that his parents had died, but Hayley found out that he had a brother who had died recently, but his sister, Vera, was still living in Becklesfield. That was Abigail though; she had her faults, but if you were her friend, there wouldn't be anything she wouldn't do for you. Terry wondered how someone who looked like Abigail had never found true love in life. Mind you, he thought, there were times when he knew exactly why. With her blonde hair, pretty face, blue eyes, and her own beguiling smile, she could always get around him, and he thought the world of her, most of the time.

Hayley interrupted his thoughts. "Did the forensics find a weapon or anything else?"

Terry had to jump in quickly before Abigail answered. "They got a metal bar that was lying there and you could see the blood on it. Plus there were various snack wrappers and a plastic water bottle floating, of course. Why the hell are they everywhere these days? I don't think we were all dying of thirst in my day. Can't people go anywhere without one, for God's sake? It's not like there aren't a million coffee places now if you want a drink. They'll find one of those bottles on the moon when we go back there, you wait and see. Sorry, where was I? And there was a short bit of thin rope. Well, I suppose there would be by the river. A piece of paper that had most of the writing washed off it, and there was a baseball hat. I didn't see where they found that, though."

"Tom can tell me tonight, hun. The bend in the river would have hidden the actual murderer from the crowds, but they'll have to question everyone to see if they saw him walking up here, or if they saw anyone else. We can leave that to the uniforms."

Abigail added, "The ground was very dry, so I don't think they will be able to find any footprints. They were still checking when I left."

"Do you want me to drive us back to Becklesfield?" asked Hayley.

Abigail pursed her lips. "Not yet. I was thinking we could go to the clubhouse and see if there is one of those wooden plaques with all the names of the club members on, to give us an idea of who's who. Nobody can see us, Hayl, but it might be a bit awkward for you."

"No probs, hun. I'll try and strike up conversations with the spectators before they all go. Shall we meet at the car in about an hour's time? I daren't try talking to Tom with Johnson around. He hates my guts."

"He'll be in the bar, you mark my words."

"I told Caroline we'll meet at my place at about ten o'clock tomorrow morning. I'll have got all the info off Tom by then."

"Okay. See you later. Come on, Betty, let's go and see if there are any more young rowers who look guilty."

"Good idea. We can kill two birds with one bush," agreed Betty.

Chapter 4

Tom had been looking out for Hayley, but he didn't see her, so made his way towards the hospitality area where three stewards were standing. As soon as they saw the good-looking young policeman in uniform, a tall man in a blazer, with a huge bushy beard, made a beeline for him.

"Officer, we heard Leo Spencer has had an accident, is that right?"

"And you are?"

"Ben Manson, racing officer. Only we've still got to have the women's coxless four, and then the raft race for the kids."

"I can't confirm it's an accident, but I can say that there'll be no more races today, sir. And once we've taken statements everyone can go."

"That is disappointing; the children have put such a lot of effort into making their rafts. What about the prizegiving? Can that go ahead?"

"I don't see why not. But don't make a big thing about it. Keep it low key, please."

"Alright, we'll do that now. We were going to have it over there, but I expect we could do it in the club with just the winners. Has anyone seen Rupert? He's in charge of the trophies and cups."

"And if you could put out on the tannoy that we don't want anyone to leave yet, it would be appreciated. Also, can you tell me where I might find Mrs Spencer, please?"

"Poor Ruth. I saw her about an hour ago, I think she went to the clubhouse, but she could be anywhere now. She'll be absolutely devastated."

"Thank you, sir. So if you could tell everyone to stay, and if you could sort out somewhere that we can speak to anyone that knew Mr Spencer personally, DCI Johnson would appreciate it. Perhaps one of the rooms in the clubhouse." Ben Manson told him that he could use the committee room, and then walked back to the others, who were also dressed in the sailing colours. They would all have to be interrogated by Johnson. They'll love that, thought Tom.

Every other person that he walked past tried to get him to say what had happened, but in the end he reached the large marina that had moorings for ten motor cruisers. He had noticed there were others on the riverbank when he had walked along the towpath once, but they were elsewhere today to make room for the races. The shop, 'Jack's Chandlery', was actually a converted wooden shed by the looks of it, and not joined on to the large modern building that housed the sailing club, the changing rooms and showers. He walked past the tables outside the sliding doors, with umbrellas to shade them from the heat on the terrace. Every seat was taken and they all turned to look at him. Inside, the bar was not as full as Tom would have imagined, but then everyone wanted to be out in the sun. A large balding man and a mousy-looking lady were serving behind the bar and they were able to say that they thought Ruth Spencer might still be in her husband's office. They had seen her go that way and not noticed her leave anyway, but she could have gone out the back door, through the kitchen.

Tom opened a door marked 'Private' and stopped outside the one with the sign for the commodore. He was about to knock, but the noise he heard stopped him. Moaning and kissing, was that? Bit awkward, he thought, but Tom still knocked. He had to smile to himself as it went suddenly quiet, and he then heard a frenzy of activity.

"Just a minute," said a female voice.

"It's the police, ma'am. I need to have a word." Again there was a deathly silence and then whispering and movement.

"Come in." Tom was surprised to see Mrs Spencer sitting behind a desk and a small, red-faced man sitting on a sofa by the window, as if they had been having a business meeting. Ruth Spencer was a beautiful woman with high cheekbones who was smoothing down her long golden hair.

"Are you Leo Spencer's wife?"

"Yes, I'm Ruth. This is my friend, Rupert Cox. We've just been, er, organising the trophies and medals for the prizegiving. What can I do for you…?"

"Police Constable Bennett. I'm sorry to tell you that your husband has had an accident."

Rupert got to his feet. "Oh my God. Is he okay?"

"I'm afraid not, sir. He was pulled from the river and pronounced dead." It was a good job that Ruth Spencer was sitting as she physically crumpled in her seat. Her face lost all colour and Rupert ran to put his arm around her.

"Leave me alone, you idiot." He removed his hand as if he had been stung. Despair and guilt were etched on her face. "Can I see him? I need to see him."

"Not at the moment. It's a crime scene."

"What crime? I thought you said it was an accident."

"Any death has to be investigated, Mrs Spencer. I'm so sorry for your loss. Detective Chief Inspector Johnson is in charge of the investigation and will need to talk to you and ask some questions. Will you excuse me while I let him know where you are? Both stay here, please."

Tom left the room to put a call through to his boss. He'd be happy. A murder victim's wife, caught with her lover! He'd probably have her arrested within the hour.

He entered the bar and was pleased to see that DCI Johnson was there and talking to the barman. Not enquiring about the victim, he realised as he got closer, but asking what was his best beer.

"Sir, I've found Ruth Spencer, the wife. She's in his office and hadn't heard the news. Mainly because she wasn't on her own. She was engaged in, how can I say this?"

"Not hanky panky?"

"Yes, that's about it. She said they were organising the cups."

"I bet he bloody was," said Johnson. He turned to the barman again. "How long has the commodore's wife been knocking it off with…"

"Rupert Cox, sir."

"Very apt. With Mr Cox? Was Rupert bare? You know, Rupert the Bear?" he retorted, laughing out loud at his own joke. But he felt old when no one else had ever heard of the character that he used to watch on television when he was young.

"You didn't hear it from me, but I've seen her getting on his boat all summer," said the barman.

The lady behind the bar had been sidling over to listen and butted in. "Since last year. I just happen to know that Cox and his wife moved his thirty-six footer from Henley to our marina at the beginning of the season. I heard it had got too expensive on the Thames for them, so he chose the River Gore. But I reckon it was so he could be closer to his fancy woman. He's always in here flaunting his cash. Not that I'm one to notice these things or gossip. I keep myself to myself, Inspector," she added and went to serve someone. The barman rolled his eyes and smiled.

Johnson sniggered. "I bet she's a right nosy old busybody. Who is the old bat?"

"My wife. And she's not old," he answered as he pulled a pint of beer and looked daggers at the mouthy policeman.

"Oops. No offence, sir. Just my little joke. I'll still need your names though."

"Barry and Moira Potts. We run the club and live in the flat upstairs."

"Take the names down, Bennett. Is there a room we can use for questioning anyone that knew him? Starting with the lovebirds. We might get home before dark, after all. Didn't I say it would be the wife?"

"You did, sir. There's the committee room. It's through that door, second on the right."

Barry said, "I couldn't believe it when someone said Leo was dead. I don't understand it. He could swim like a fish. Did he trip or something? It's not going to look good for the club."

"What sort of bloke was he?"

"Life and soul most of the time. Always pleasant and the ladies liked him. He could rub some of the other committee members up the wrong way because he was so laid back. It's the second death we've had at the regatta that I know about. About four years ago, one of the rowers had a heart attack, but he wasn't with Ottersmill."

"Sounds like a dangerous hobby then. Look, Barry, I haven't got time for a pint, so make it a quick snifter. Your best scotch, barman and put it on my tab." Bennett had never seen him pay for a drink yet when he was on a case.

"We might as well get your statement out of the way first, where were you and your beautiful wife for the last few hours?"

"Stuck behind here, give or take, or collecting the glasses from the tables and outside," said Barry.

Moira Potts had heard the question from the other end of the bar while pouring a prosecco, and must have ears like a bat, Tom noticed. "The only time I got a break was when I had to grab my old bucket and mop to clear up when someone came to tell me that one of the young rowers had a few too many, and threw up in the girls' cloakroom."

"That's right. She was only gone for a few minutes. It's a wonder more people don't end up dead in the river with all the drinks we've served," added Barry. "There's Champagne and Pimms served from first thing in the morning in the marquees as well."

"You're off the hook for now then; so I'll let you serve me. Phone Sergeant Mills, Bennett, and tell him to meet me there. Let the widow and Rupert the Bear stew for a while. But separate them before they can concoct an alibi and make up a story. Put her in the committee room and leave him where he is for now. You better stay with him though. Me and this fine single malt are going to get acquainted first."

Johnson was actually on his second when Abigail, Terry and Betty entered the clubhouse - drinking doubles, of course. Although he couldn't see them, they were pleased when he left through the door marked 'Private'. In the corner of the room they were just in time to see Lady Caroline presenting the trophy to the winners of the Hatton Challenge Cup.

Betty nudged Abigail and pointed to the tall, strong man in lycra that they had seen earlier getting out of his racing boat. He was presented with the cup, along with another man, and they learned his name was David MacIntosh.

"He can MacIn my tosh anyday," said Betty.

"My tush too," said Abigail dreamily. "I mean tosh."

"Oh, put your eyes back in your head, you two, for goodness' sake."

"For your information, Terry, I was investigating."

"Looked more like drooling to me."

"I was trying to see if he was left-handed, actually."

"And is he?"

"I don't know. I haven't got to his hands yet. But I'm getting there. Er, he's right-handed, going by his watch. But I could do some under the covers, sorry, undercover surveillance to make sure. I'm joking, Terry. Okay, come on, Betty, let's go and look at the board over there. So, the Vice Commodore is Gail Fletcher. Treasurer is Ruth Spencer – that's very interesting. Racing Officer is Benjamin Manson. Secretary is Karen Perkins. The Club Steward is Barry Potts."

"Look at this poster, Abigail," said Betty. "It says the sailing and rowing instructors are Nina Moore and David MacIntosh."

Abigail sighed. "It's days like this I wish I was alive, Betty. And a few years younger."

"Just a few," scoffed Terry. "Try fifteen."

"Bit harsh, Terry. But that does mean that he would have known Leo, and so we'll have to keep a watchful eye on him, Betty. Hayley had better question him, lucky girl. Let's go and see what Johnson is up to now."

The three spirits walked through two doors until they found Mills and the DCI sitting at a long table, opposite a lady with red eyes and dabbing at them with a tissue. Whether this was due to Johnson's questioning or she was the grieving widow they were yet to find out. They weren't expecting the next question, as even for Johnson it felt a bit cruel.

"So you say you're upset about your husband's death and how much you loved him, but you still were caught bonking with your boyfriend in an office before he was even cold."

"We weren't bonking. Kissing at most. I did love Leo."

"About as much as my wife loved me before the divorce, I'd say, Mrs Spencer."

"Our lives are complicated. We both have our own businesses and he spent most of the weekends here in the summer.

I'm the treasurer and when Leo was made commodore we saw even less of each other. And Mr Cox isn't my boyfriend."

"I've heard you've been seeing your fancy man since last year, even before he moved his huge boat here."

"Rubbish. It was a one-off."

"Getting it off, I heard," said Johnson, laughing at his own joke again. "Look, we're going to need you to write a statement of what you got up to all day today. All of your movements. And the times. From when you got here first thing this morning. Did you arrive together?"

"No. We always come in separate cars. Leo likes to stay later than me and drink in the bar. I'd rather get home. It's only a fifteen-minute drive from here."

"When was the last time you saw your husband?"

"We had a bit of lunch in the hospitality tent at about one o'clock. So I didn't see him after quarter to two. I watched the racing for a while and then met Rupert here at about quarter past three. What time did it happen?"

"We don't know yet. But I think you're going to need a better alibi than Rupert Cox, put it that way. You'll need to come to Gorebridge Police Station and write a formal statement and sign it tomorrow, but you can go home now, Mrs Spencer. We'll be talking to Mr Cox next. See her out and go and fetch him, Sergeant."

Unheard by the two policemen and the widow, Abigail, Betty and Terry all talked at once.

"Well, that's a new one," said Betty. "Caught with your boyfriend when they find your husband's body. By the police as well."

"Very unlucky, I'd say," said Abigail.

"Johnson will think all his birthdays have come in one day," added Terry. "I'm beginning to think I should have got a boat when I was alive. It's all going on here, isn't it?"

Abigail sighed. "Tell me about it. What a missed opportunity. Sailing, single men and sex. Sounds like a good title for a book."

They didn't have time to talk about regrets as Mills was showing in Rupert Cox. He wasn't Abigail's type though. She preferred dark, handsome and preferably younger. His thin mousy hair was receding fast and he looked to be in his fifties. Although, going by his clothes and watch, he seemed to be pretty rich. Maybe that was the attraction.

Johnson rubbed his hands together and looked like a lion about to leap on his prey, while the suspect looked like the gazelle who knew his fate.

"Sit down, sir. So you are Rupert Cox?"

"Yes. I live in Henley, Inspector."

"Very nice, I'm sure. And it's Detective Chief Inspector."

"In that case, it's Rupert Cox KC. That means King's Counsel if you didn't know."

"It makes no difference to me, son. Tell him, Sergeant Mills."

Mills shook his head. "No, it really doesn't, sir. My boss treats everyone the same. Rich or poor."

"Very true. I hate everyone. And lawyers the most. You make a career out of telling lies. So how will we know when you are telling the truth? And I have to tell you that Leo Spencer was murdered earlier, and you are the most likely suspect."

"I'd never kill anyone. Especially not a friend."

"Some friend you are. Having it off with his wife in the middle of his regatta."

"We were not having it off, as you crudely put it. We were canoodling at most."

"Canoodling doesn't sound much better to me. Where's your wife today, Mr Cox?"

"My wife doesn't like the boating scene. She only comes when she has friends to entertain and impress. She likes me to take them for a cruise on the river, while she sits on the back knocking back the wine."

"So you're free to see your bit on the side."

"She's not just that. We're in love."

"That's not what she told us. According to others, you were her fancy man." Johnson looked him up and down and added, "In the loosest term, I guess."

"Really, Inspector, I didn't come here to be insulted."

"Call it an extra bonus. So why did she deny you were her lover?"

"If Ruth did deny our love then it must be the grief talking, or she didn't want to look…"

"Guilty?"

"Yes. It obviously looks a bit fishy for both of us."

"I'd say about as fishy as a trout that swallowed a mackerel, sir."

Rupert held up his hands. "She can hardly add that he was a useless husband that had affairs, drank too much and spent far too much time with the young sailing cadets. I could give you a list of reasons that someone might have wanted Leo dead."

Mills and Johnson exchanged looks. "Well, when you come to Gorebridge Police Station tomorrow you can fill us in. Are you right-handed, Sir?"

"Just answer the question, please," added Mills.

"Left. What of it?"

"We think the attacker was left-handed. What would a lawyer say to that?"

"A good lawyer would say that ten percent of the world's population are left-handed. So considering there were maybe a thousand people here today, he would say that means that one hundred people could be guilty."

"But how many of them were sleeping with the victim's wife? So I don't need your Oxbridge qualification to tell you that the answer has gone down to one. Or maybe there were others for all you know. So can you account for your whereabouts this afternoon? And yes, I'll need a better alibi than your mistress."

Abigail noticed how quickly it had gone from an interview to an interrogation.

"I can't think. I was in and out of all the marquees. I watched the races with a few people. Ben Manson and Gail, the VC, amongst others. I saw Ruth after three and we decided to come to the office. And the rest you know."

"Yes, and I wish I didn't. How did you know that Leo wouldn't come back here and catch you? Was it because you'd sent him on a wild goose chase? Or should I say a wild swan chase. Or did you know he was already dead, and so you needed to be seen coming here by everybody? It was bad luck for you that the little lad just happened to find the body, wasn't it? If it was simply means, motive and opportunity, we've got you bang to rights. But you'd know that being a KC, m'lord."

"Having an affair is hardly a motive. Divorce works just as well these days."

"You might find out how well that works, sir. I'm guessing you've got to go home to your wife and give her the news. I don't envy you one bit. You might need a lawyer, or a doctor yourself," Johnson laughed. "Write down your name and address before you go, and we're going to need to examine what you and Mrs Spencer are wearing today. If we see one speck of blood, you've had it."

Rupert got to his feet. "You will find no evidence, and I can assure you that I will have the best defence that money can buy."

Abigail got to her feet as Rupert left. "Poor man. He's in for a hard time. He looks as white as a sheet. One minute you're with the woman of your dreams, then the next minute you're with a man from your nightmares."

"But what do we think?" asked Terry. "Guilty or not guilty?"

"I don't think he would have the nerve. He looked a bit weaselly to me. More a stab in the back or rat poison in his dinner than facing him head-on. You'd have to really hate someone to do that, and he doesn't look the type. Don't you agree, Abigail?"

"That's a very good point, Betty. But look, he's left-handed. Even Johnson noticed that. He sure has put the fear of God in him. I wonder if he'll even dare tell his wife about Ruth Spencer. The murder will be all over the news soon, so he won't have to tell her that. But if he doesn't tell her about his girlfriend, Johnson will be delighted to."

"Poor man. And of course Johnson is such an idiot, that he's bound to arrest him, guilty or not," said Terry.

"What's that saying about a fool?" said Betty, deep in thought. "It's on the slip of my tongue."

"Tip," Abigail corrected her.

"Yes, please."

Abigail smiled. "Okay. Hmm, you can fool the people some of the time?"

"No."

"Er, I know, better to remain silent and be thought a fool?"

"No," as Betty waved her hand dismissively.

"Fool me once, shame on me? Fools rush in?"

"No, that's not it," Betty said impatiently.

"Suffer fools gladly? A fool and his money?" Abigail sighed.

Betty thought for a moment. "I know. Dumber than a box of socks!"

"Seriously, Betty?" said Abigail. "Well that's ten minutes I'll never get back," she whispered to Terry.

"You got that right, Betty. Johnson is a fool in any language," said Terry. "I've had enough of this room. I don't think we're going to get any more clues until we know who is who. We might as well let the police do their job and get all the names and times. Tom can pass it on to Hayley for us. Shall we have a quick nose around the club before we go and meet Hayley?"

"We might as well while we're here. Let's see what's upstairs first." They followed Abigail up a steep staircase that led to a door marked 'No Admittance'. Not for them, though, as they walked through it into a small sitting room, which led to an even smaller bedroom and galley-style kitchen.

"I wonder who lives here?" said Betty.

"Going by the photo over there, I'm guessing the two behind the bar. At least they don't have to commute, I suppose. I wonder how long they've lived here. One of them likes murder mystery books and they've got a nice view of the river," said Terry. "There are worse places to live, even if it is on the small side."

"We should come back when they're here and listen to what they are talking about. I bet if one of them did it, the other one would have known. Let's look at the other rooms downstairs." The first one they came to was the dead man's office.

"So this is where the commodore does his thing," said Abigail.

"And where his wife does her thing from the sound of it," added Terry. "I hope Tom knocked."

"There's a key on the inside, so I'm hoping they locked it. But they must have known that Leo was busy."

"Or dead," said Betty.

"Precisely. Did they know? I'll check on his desk," said Abigail. "There's a list of boats for sale. Something about moorings. Look, there's a phone number next to the letter F, with a Gorebridge code. Sergeant Mills will check that out, I'm sure, in case that's who got Leo to meet them. Look, he's like me, he likes doodling."

"Or canoodling like Rupert," joked Betty.

"He probably does, but I mean like this." Abigail pointed to a bit of paper about the regatta which had boxes and spirals on it. "I used to do this when I was on the phone. He must have had a lot of calls recently. I used to do flowers sometimes. There are boxes all joined together; that was my favourite. I used to put crosses in them. Then he's gone on to spirals. Now, the last lot he's done are stars."

"What does that mean, dear?"

"Well, I'm not a psychologist, Terry, stop that, but I think the stars mean that he's happy."

"That's a bit of a stretch, isn't it?" said Terry.

"Probably. But it might mean something. I did flowers and he did stars."

"Well, my mind must be normal because I never did that."

Abigail nudged Betty. "That's because phones weren't invented in your day."

"Cheeky monkey. This might be a bit more useful," said Terry. "A VHF radio that they can talk to the boats on. Maybe he heard something on there that got him killed."

"If the murderer called him on the radio for the meeting, then there won't be anything to trace back to him or her. Unless he wrote it down."

"Logged," said Terry. "What? You're not the only one who knows things, Abigail Summers."

Betty was looking out of the window. "He's got a nice view from here." The boats that were out of the water were in the front next to the boat sheds and beyond that was the River Gore. "He might have seen a drug deal gone wrong." Betty always mentioned that scenario, but she hadn't been right yet.

"Yes. He could well have seen something he shouldn't have, and got killed for it."

Terry said, "It's no good guessing, we'll check out the rest of the place and go back, shall we?"

They went to check out the small cloakrooms, which were full of men in one and girls in the other, getting out of their rowing gear, so Terry covered Abigail's eyes in the men's.

Finally, they went through another 'Private' door that went into a small kitchen, which led to an outside yard. On the left was some metal junk, a pile of old clothes, a bike and some gardening equipment, and on the right were rubbish bins, a rickety-looking ladder and wooden crates that were half-full of empty bottles. Terry stuck just his head through a gate on the far side.

"That's the lane we came on. If you go right, it takes you to the Jolly Sailor at Tingleford. You turn left for Becklesfield and Hayley's Mini is down there. Shall we go and wait there for her?"

Betty was the first to answer him. "Oh, yes please. I love a day out, but there's nothing like getting home to the peace and tranquillity of Becklesfield Public Library. Especially on a Sunday when it's just us ghosts."

"You're right there, Betty," said Abigail. "I think I've spent more time with people since I've been dead than when I was alive and running my dressmaking business. I'm not sure I like most of them. Mind you, a lot of them have been murderers and blackmailers."

"Well, you know what they say," said Betty, who took an awful lot of notice of what 'they' said. But very rarely said it correctly herself. "You can choose your friends but you cannot choose your enemies."

"Your family, Betty," Abigail pointed out.

"What about them, dear?"

"You can't choose them."

"I would."

"No, I just meant that we… Help me out, Terry."

Terry shook his head. "Sometimes, I don't know what you're talking about, Abigail," he joked. "Come on, ladies, we haven't got all day to chat."

Chapter 5

IN THE SUPPOSED SAFETY OF A LUXURIOUS PENTHOUSE apartment in Knightsbridge, Adreena Van Derson turned down the volume of her television set and sat up straight. It had followed her here. Her heart started to pound and she found it hard to breathe. Why was it happening again? Early that morning, as soon as it had got light, she had driven up to stay in the family's London townhouse. She had to get away as fast as she could, knowing there would be a strong security presence in the lobby and even a panic room if she needed it.

The attractive, twenty-six-year-old was sitting in her peach satin pyjamas, on the antique, olive-green sofa. And although she had left in a hurry, in fear of her life, her chestnut hair and make-up were still immaculate.

Adreena had left her home on the Brighton seafront when she couldn't bear it any longer. There, Adreena had felt exposed and alone. For the first year, she was so happy in the Regency, white-pillared building, where she could sit all day looking out of her third-floor apartment at the sea. There were plenty of places to eat out and she'd never been so content. For once, she could be herself and do exactly as she pleased. Adreena had even fired her personal maid so she could be on her own for the first time in her life. Of course, she had hired a local housekeeper to come in and cook and clean for her during the day. No one would expect her to do that sort of thing. The location was the best in Brighton, as it was near to the marina where Daddy had kept the yacht. Not that it had been used since he had died. Perhaps they should sell it. Her brother, Casper, wasn't interested in sailing either, but it could be handy for business trips in the future.

Then it had all started. First, it was the doorbell ringing and no one was there. She'd put that down to children being children. What wasn't so easily explained was the noises, shadows and even the bad dreams. Then things started disappearing. Small things like her keys or her phone, that then appeared when she turned her back. More terrifying was the three knocks that she heard as soon as she got in bed and seemed to come from the other side of the room. The thud of footsteps she really tried to convince herself were coming from above or below, although in truth they seemed to be following her around the large apartment. That morning she had walked into the kitchen to find that every cupboard door and drawer was open, so someone had been there while she was vulnerable in her bed. The strange thing was, that nothing ever happened when Mrs Parr, the housekeeper, was there. She was hoping that her fiancé, Lewis, would come and look after her, but as usual, he had to work. So she had no choice; that was as much as she could take. She was leaving.

So Adreena packed a suitcase and headed to London to stay in the building that Daddy had bought, mainly for business reasons. She tried to put it down to vibrations when a photo of her parents, in an ornate silver frame, had fallen down. But after all the lights had flickered and the floorboards creaked with steps from an unseen person coming towards her, she knew whoever or whatever it was had pursued her to London.

She didn't move off the sofa but turned the sound up loudly with shaky hands. She couldn't bring herself to get the burly security guard to come up. What could she say that wouldn't make her sound like an idiot? She needed to be with other people and then she would have a witness to this cowardly enemy.

Adreena relaxed as she made a decision. The Van Dersons had a large country house, Luxborough Grange. Her cousin, Viktor, lived there with his family and it was once her childhood home. It was always busy with maids, gardeners and even old Scrivens, the butler. You were lucky to get any privacy, which at the time was one of the reasons that she had left. She turned every light on and decided to watch television all night, so she grabbed a throw and settled herself on the sofa. She would contact the town chauffeur to drive her down to Lux in the morning. Adreena Van Derson sighed with relief that this time tomorrow, she'd be back in Becklesfield.

Chapter 6

"Morning, Hayley, here's a nice cup of tea. I've fed the cat," said Tom.

Hayley spoke from under the cover. "Thanks, hun. What time is it?"

"Just gone seven. There's a big meeting at eight about the murder. The Chief Constable will be there, so I can't be late. You know he always appears when someone rich is murdered. You go back to sleep, darling."

"You must be tired. You had a long shift yesterday and then you had to tell me all the news." Hayley sat up and leaned on one arm. "I've got a lot to tell the others this morning. I wonder what Johnson will do today."

"Probably nothing. But some of us will have to go back to Ottersmill and do a search again. Either that, or do a search of Leo Spencer's house. There's a list as long as your arm of who we have to talk to and get more times and places and all that. There must have been over five hundred people there yesterday. I'd put a bet on that it was someone he knew, though. What else would he be doing up that part of the river? But we have to show his picture and the two lovers' photos to try and get an idea of where they were."

"I don't envy you at all. Sounds very time consuming and boring. I might learn something from the others. But it's not all spirits today, hun, Lady Caroline is coming. She knows Ruth Spencer, and I daresay some of the others."

"Well, you be careful, Hayley. Go back to sleep for a while. I'll see you tonight." He bent down to kiss his wife of three years on top of her head as she sipped her tea, then left for work.

But little Luna, the tortoiseshell kitten, had other ideas. Hayley had rescued him from certain death when Abigail was led to him by his mother, Tiggy, who had died. She wrapped him up in her cardigan and brought him home, and somehow he had survived. Now Luna was awake and full of energy, so Hayley should be. After ten minutes of being jumped on, walked over and having her face sat on, she gave up. The final straw was when he used her long black hair as a ball of wool to paw at. After getting dressed and feeding the obviously starving cat, who hadn't been fed for at least an hour, Hayley took a bowl of cereal into the conservatory.

Satisfied that his owner was now awake and downstairs to see to his every need, Luna took up his favourite spot on the windowsill and went back to sleep. But Hayley suddenly realised that she had better tidy up a bit. She'd never had a Lady visit before.

"It's alright for you, Luna, you can sleep all day. I'd better dust and hoover before she comes. And I can't give her a mug. I'd better find out those cups and saucers. And use a teapot. Oh God, I haven't got a teapot. I gave it to the charity shop. Oh, she'll never know, I'll just dip a tea bag in her cup in the kitchen. Damn, I've only got those cheap biscuits, and I ate most of them last night. Oh, Luna, what am I worrying about that for? It's going to be total chaos with the spirits talking and me relaying it all to Caroline, and Abigail never shutting up long enough. It'll be fine," she told herself. So she decided to sit down for five minutes and fell back asleep.

It wasn't fine! Hayley woke up and looked around her living room to see what she thought might happen - utter chaos. Luckily, Lady Caroline hadn't arrived yet. The entire Deadly Detective Agency was there. All talking at once.

"Quiet! I see why a poltergeist means a noisy ghost now. They've got nothing on you lot, if you don't mind me saying."

"Sorry, Hayley," said Abigail. "Were you asleep?"

"Not anymore, hun. Don't tell me you're all dying to know what Tom had to say."

"Bit harsh, but true."

"Okay. Make yourselves at home, but I'll keep most of the juicy stuff for when Caroline gets here." Hayley smiled at Lillian and Suzie. "I'm so pleased you both came. How are your mother and brother, Suzie?" Suzie was a beautiful black girl who had been killed by a drunk driver when she was nine. At the hospital, Lillian Yin had taken her on as her own. She was still in her nurse's uniform as she had died after a long shift in the Children's Ward.

"We spent the day watching over them yesterday, so that was nice. It's just a shame that we missed all the fun at the regatta."

Hayley told them what she had learned from Tom, and the others filled them in on the interviews with Rupert and Ruth.

"Tom said that Johnson had a near falling out with the husband and wife behind the bar. Moira Potts is only thirty or forty, but Johnson managed to call her a nosy old bat."

"He has a way with words, for sure. With him, that's grounds enough for an arrest," added Betty.

Terry shook his head. "I'm putting my money on the wife and her boyfriend being his first choice."

Betty said, "I wonder if his murder was a chance thing, or if it was prenom, predominated, premetiated - planned."

Abigail said, "I think it was premeninated, prenedimated, calculated, Betty. He must have been there to meet someone, but it might not have been those two. Or not necessarily both of them."

Hayley suddenly closed her eyes and held up her finger. "Lady Caroline is here."

Betty put her hand on her heart. "I think it's amazing how you do that. Do you feel a sensation, or see a vision?"

"No, Betty. I heard the car door slam," she laughed, as she stood up to go and open the front door.

"Come in, Caroline. The gang's all here, so it may be a bit chaotic, for me anyway. Now, you've met Abigail," she said as she pointed towards the empty chairs. "Next to her is Betty, Terry and over there is young Suzie and Lillian."

"Ah, the nurse. I've heard all about you. Tell me if I'm about to sit on anyone, won't you? And Suzie, I'd love to see your excellent skills that I've been told about. I hear you're an excellent Haunter and Mover."

On cue, Suzie picked up a cushion and put it in the back of an empty chair that was reserved for the visitor.

"Thank you, Suzie," said Hayley. "Please take a seat, Caroline. Now that all the introductions are over, shall we begin? Look, it's no good you talking all at once. Don't forget our guest can't hear a word. Thank you. I'll just give a quick roundup then you can all join in."

Abigail crossed her arms and sulked. It should be her telling everyone, not Hayley. There were definitely more disadvantages than advantages in being dead. It was hard for her to keep quiet at the best of times, let alone when there was a murder to solve. But she let Hayley take over her role—for now.

"Okay then. Now, Leo Spencer was with his wife, Ruth, having lunch in the VIP refreshment marquee from about one o'clock till about half past. We know the body was found about three-thirty by Jacob Redman, upstream, away from the regatta. It was around a bend in the river and so far no one has admitted to seeing anybody go up there. Not Leo, the boy or the killer. So there's a couple of hours to find out about. Tom says that they've got a list of people to talk to, so that will help. Or maybe he was dead the whole time. They still don't know why he went to that part of the river, but chances are, it was to meet someone. But was that prearranged, or did he get a note, call or text just before? His phone is still missing."

"Could be anywhere in the river."

"Yes. As Terry just said, Caroline, it could be at the bottom of the river, or taken away by the current. You may not know this, but Ruth was with her lover, Rupert Cox, having you-know-what when Tom found her in her husband's office to notify her of his death."

"No. I don't believe it. I would never have thought it of her. Leo, yes, but not her. Isn't Rupert that skinny chap that has something to do with the racing? I have a feeling I met him in the morning. That gives them a motive, but surely to goodness they wouldn't be so stupid as to get caught on the very day of the murder."

"Precisely. Although, it does make for an unforgettable alibi, doesn't it? They said they were together in the office from just after three o'clock. So either or both could have lured him up there in person. So there would be nothing on their phones; which I'm sure they will check. And is adultery really a reason these days for murder? Divorce is far easier, unless Ruth stood to lose a fortune."

Caroline shook her head. "She owns Cranston Stables, which must be worth a small fortune. It's been in the family for years and it stands on a lot of ground. Mind you, it could be running at a loss, but I haven't heard it is. I meet up with a few of horse's owners sometimes to discuss the gymkhana that's happening at Chiltern Hall next year. Are there any other suspects apart from them?"

"I suppose there's the Vice Commodore, Gail Fletcher. She gets the top spot now, but would she want the job that badly? Ben Manson let himself be known to Tom and wanted to know what was going on. He knew Leo well and could have had a reason. Barry and Moira Potts run the bar, and until they've been questioned properly we won't know if they had it in for him. And by all accounts they were stuck behind the bar all day."

Abigail really tried but she couldn't be quiet any longer. "Ask her if she knows David MacIntosh."

So Hayley did but Lady Caroline frowned and didn't think that she did. "Is he a person of interest?"

Betty and Abigail said he definitely was and Hayley said, "Let's just say us girls fancy him for it, bun, I mean hun," as Terry groaned.

"He wouldn't be the Adonis that won the coxless doubles, would he? Actually don't answer that. Yes, I do know him. Not well, unfortunately. But when I gave him the Hatton Challenge Cup, I couldn't help but have a good look at him. I do know the name though, now I think of it. Not as well as a lot of the ladies in the county. I'm surprised you don't, Hayley."

"I don't think I would forget him, hun."

"Thinking about it, he would be a more likely candidate to be hit on the head and thrown in the river than Leo. He's what used to be called a gigolo."

"What's a gigglow?" asked Suzie.

Hayley answered. "A gigolo, Suzie, is a good-looking man who is paid by wealthy women to provide a kind of service. And he must make a fortune."

"Oh, you mean like plumbing or gardening. I'm kidding,"

laughed Suzie, as a relieved Hayley was wondering how on earth she could explain it to the young girl.

Caroline told them, "They say he's got a fancy apartment in Gorebridge, paid for by one of his clients. I could guess by who, but I'm not at liberty to say. But I know quite a few of the older ladies are rather friendly with him. So I should imagine there would be quite a few husbands after him."

"I've gone right off him now," said Betty. "Mainly because I could never have afforded him. Not only that, I never liked sharing my chocolates when I was alive, I sure wouldn't want to share a man. Anyway, my John and I had plenty of excitement in that way. Did I tell you that he liked a good…?"

Hayley jumped in fast. "Yes, thank you, I believe you did tell us, hun. And don't forget it wouldn't be fair to leave Caroline out of the conversation. I wonder how many of the sailing club he was seeing on the side. But then it wasn't him that was murdered. Unless he killed Leo for some other reason."

Abigail agreed. "Abigail is saying it could be blackmail, as we know it happens a lot in these small villages, where everyone knows everyone's business. If Leo knew something that would put the ladies off David, then that would do it. He would stand to lose his flat and a load of money. Caroline, I don't suppose you know what sort of business Leo had, do you?"

"He started selling electric bikes a few years ago. A lot of people own one. Makes a fortune by all accounts. They're sold all over Europe as well now. I've got one myself. The make is, um, what's the advert? 'Estryke Bikes - Go where you like'."

"Is that him? Mind you, I feel safer in my little Mini. Lillian says do you know where they live?"

"I do. They live in that luxury gated community, Edenbury Heights. It's between Becklesfield and Ottersmill. Very select. There's only about five houses there. I don't know the name or number of Ruth's house, but it's known as the glass house, so maybe Leo threw stones. The other houses are huge as well. I know a footballer lives there, two doctors, who are husband and wife, another family that I've never met and Heather Lockwood, if you've heard of her."

"The TV chef that used to be on that daytime show and writes those cookery books?" asked Hayley.

"That's her, yes. I can't remember if she ever married. Or maybe she's divorced or something, but she lives on her own, I know that. She donates her books to some of the charities I help. I don't like to sleuth and run, everybody, but I need to get going. I have a meeting with the committee for the Charity Fun Run next month. And, if I'm honest, it is a bit strange being here with all you spirits. I hope you won't mind if I get to my next appointment." Abigail was overjoyed but didn't say. Maybe now she could get a word in edgeways. "Is there anything more I can do to help, Hayley?"

"We might need you to drop in on Ruth at one point, Caroline. Pay your condolences or something."

"I can't see why not. I've met her once or twice at the gymkhana meetings. And while I'm there, I could drop in and see Heather Lockwood to thank her for the books or ask her to sign one for a charity auction. She might have some gossip on her neighbour. Although I would imagine that the murder has more to do with the boat fraternity than his neighbours, myself."

"I'm sure Abigail and the others would agree. But it doesn't hurt to check. She might know something about Leo that no one else does. Thank you so much for coming, Caroline. I'll see you out."

After they had all said their goodbyes and Hayley had returned, she suddenly realised teapot or no teapot, she had completely forgotten to offer her distinguished guest a cup of tea. Oh well, too late now. "That must have been hard for you, Abigail, to not be able to talk and give your opinion, hun."

"Not at all. I never thought that for a second."

"More like half an hour, I reckon," said Terry.

"Haha. I thought you handled it perfectly, Hayley."

"Why, that's high praise from you."

"Although," whereupon all the others smiled at each other. Although and but were two words they didn't like to hear at the beginning of a sentence from Abigail. "I would have asked her why she would have believed it of Leo to have cheated, but not Ruth. She must know something. And I would have got a list of those that Caroline suspected of seeing David MacIntosh, and the one who had bought him his flat. And I… but you did very well."

"We can't all be as, what's the word?"

"Brilliant? Intuitive? Perfect?" suggested Abigail.

"No. I was thinking of dominating," smiled Hayley, who was often too soft for her own good.

"I can think of a few myself," agreed Terry as he winked at Betty.

But Betty said, "There's nothing wrong with being dominating. If you remember, my John used to love it when I put on my black …"

"I think we all remember that," said Hayley.

"The word I'm thinking of is marvellous," said Suzie, emphatically. Abigail was her hero and was always amazed at how she worked out who the murderer was, as well as any of the detectives in the mystery books that she read in Becklesfield Library.

"Thank you, Suzie. You know you're my favourite."

"So, boss, what's next?" asked Lillian. "I haven't met this David yet, if you need a volunteer."

"Not you as well. Sometimes I feel very outnumbered by the females here."

"A bit jealous, are we, Terry?" asked Abigail.

"Sounds like if you were alive, you couldn't afford him."

"I earned good money, thank you very much. And I didn't have to pay to get a boyfriend. I could have my pick of men."

"But would they pick you?" goaded Terry.

"At least I…"

"WILL YOU SHUT UP, PLEASE," shouted Hayley. "I've got a headache now. I swear you two got on better before you got together."

"We're not together," they both answered and folded their arms in unison.

"Look, how about this, I'll take Betty and Terry to the marina. They can look out for other spirits to talk to, and maybe even find the commodore wandering around in a daze. And on the way, I'll drop Abigail, Suzie and Lillian to do their thing and search Leo's house before the police get there. Abigail can snoop and sleuth, Suzie can have a good rummage around, and Lillian has a good eye for knowing what's important and what's not. I'll have to make sure Johnson isn't in Ottersmill, but I reckon he'll be interviewing the widow today, and maybe Rupert. I'll head for the club and have a drink and a chat with Moira behind the bar. Tom said she likes a good gossip and knows exactly what's going on."

"See if there's anyone there that can tell you about having sailing lessons. Especially with David or that girl. He gives a whole new meaning to the saying messing about on the river. And don't forget to pop in the chandlery and have a word with Jack, and ask about the murder weapon. You know, if he's sold any lately."

"Perhaps I should have said bossy as well. Don't worry, Abi, I will. I'm getting quite good at this, although I say it myself."

Lillian said, "I know, we all are. It's just a shame we aren't alive to reap the rewards."

"On that note, Lillian," said Hayley. "When we were walking in Ridgeway Woods yesterday and you and Suzie were at her mum's, we came up with a couple of ideas. This affects you more, Suzie. I'm thinking of adding a Deadly Detective Agency section to the website for my psychic services. Nothing too much. Just if you have any problems et cetera, and I can add our motto - All Problems Great and Small. We're not talking about murders or anything like that. Maybe lost pets, missing jewellery or even divorce cases. But if it's okay with you, Suzie, we'd like to open a bank account for your brother, Jordan, for when he goes to university."

"Really? Thank you so much. That will be less for Mum to worry about as well. I was hoping you could meet her soon anyway. Jordan was being bullied by some other boys and we think we've sorted that, but Mum still needs to know about it."

"Of course I will. I'll text her. I won't tell her that we're collecting for Jordan yet, it might seem too much like charity. And we might not make anything. Let's go in the next few days and I'll tell her whatever you want me to say. And one other thing that you and Lillian don't know, I said I'd write down the cases as we get them in a book. Just for us probably, but you never know. We're calling it The Casebook of the Deadly Detective Agency."

"I'd buy it," said Suzie. "I love any murder mysteries. Will I be in it?"

Abigail said, "Of course. We couldn't have solved any of the cases without you. You're the only one that can move things. I'd love that ability. In fact, I can't wait to get started at Leo's. I reckon now is a good time to go. Ruth will be at Gorebridge Police Station and we'll have the house to ourselves if we're quick."

Hayley sat up straight and held up a finger again.

"Another visitor arriving, dear?" asked Betty

"No, hun. This time it is a vision and a feeling of heaviness. I see a small child. A young girl with a flower in her blonde hair. A pink rose, I think. No, I lost it. She's gone."

"Who do you think she was?" asked Suzie.

"I have no idea. She looked about three or four, and she was smiling, so hopefully nothing is wrong. She may come back. Sorry, it's the downside of being psychic. Well, let's get going, folks, places to go, murders to solve." Hayley sounded happy enough, but she couldn't help but think of the pretty little girl with the flower in her hair, and the feeling that somebody, somewhere was suffering.

Chapter 7

AFTER HAYLEY HAD SOMEHOW MANAGED TO GET THE five ghosts in her small Mini, she dropped off Abigail, Suzie and Lillian outside the gates of Edenbury Heights and drove off towards the river. The three of them could only stand in awe at the five huge houses.

"Well, there's a motive that wasn't there when I was murdered," said Abigail.

"Success?"

"Thank you, Lillian. My sewing business was very successful, actually. I was just thinking of money. That must be the Spencers'. I see what they mean about the glass. Surely everyone can see in. There's more glass than bricks. I'd have made a fortune making the curtains for this place. And the window cleaner must be rich." They walked through the black wrought-iron gates, which usually you could only enter by code or by a resident, and went towards the glass house that was actually called Cedar Cottage.

"That's the biggest cottage I've ever seen," said Lillian.

From the privet hedge surrounding it, a young woman appeared and began walking back and forth. Being a dressmaker,

Abigail put her clothes to be in the eighteenth century. She stood still when she realised the three of them were looking at her.

"At last, someone can see me."

"Indeed we can. Abigail, Lillian and this is Suzie."

"Elizabeth Edenbury. Good day to you all. It's been a while since I've had someone to converse with. Actually, since the day that they dismantled my beautiful manor house brick by brick, and built these monstrosities in its place. I would leave but I'm waiting for my betrothed, Samuel, to return to me. He left to make his fortune in London at my father's behest."

Abigail frowned. "I'm not a great expert on men myself, but take it from me, Elizabeth, if he hasn't come back in three hundred years, he ain't coming, sweetheart."

"Three hundred years? Is it really that long? Surely not. I seem to have lost track of time," she said sadly.

"Maybe it's time to get on with your life or death," said Lillian kindly.

"What a lovely thought. I could see my sisters and my dearest mother again. I'm not sure how though."

"You'll know when the time comes. Look out for the light."

Abigail pushed hastily in front of Lillian, giving her a dirty look. "But before you go, could you tell us about the people who live here?"

"They're awful. Every one of them. They rush about with no decorum. And you wouldn't believe the noise they make. Life was so peaceful in my day. Those infernal metal things on wheels for a start. Then there's those boxes that they stare at incessantly. Although, I have learned many things from it. Being a girl, I was educated by a governess, Miss Milton, but she only taught me to read and write. And I can embroider a flower and cross-stitch a tapestry, for all the good it did me. But from that talking box, I've learned about the Vikings, Charles Dickens' stories and even how to makeover a house if I had one, and how to move abroad. But the music - well, if that is progress, I'm sorry, I'll take a string quartet any time. Mind you, I do like watching the residents' shenanigans. You wouldn't believe what they get up to."

"I probably would, but tell us anyway," said Abigail excitedly.

"Well, see the house with a thousand windows, which by the way, must cost them a king's ransom in taxes, well, a couple live there called Leo and Ruth. It's actually called Cedar Cottage. My grandfather planted trees from all over the world and they had the cheek to chop them down, even though they had been growing for hundreds of years. They left that big cedar, but all the redwoods and other exotic ones have all gone. Mind you, we lost five in the Great Storm of 1703. But those two don't speak much these days, mainly because he doesn't spend much time there. He goes off early in his tin on wheels and she goes off in hers about noon. Their box is usually off, so I'm not there much. And you didn't hear this from me, but sometimes another man visits the lady of the house.

Now, this house, Yew Lodge, is where the Sharmas live. They are both doctors and have a son and daughter who are about my age. Leo had a soft spot for her."

"For the wife?"

"No, for the young daughter. Over there, Ashtree House, is owned by a nice black couple and their young children. He's a businessman. Something to do with banks. The Beeches is where a footballer lives, although I have no idea what that means. His family is rather nice. Although, I did hear that they weren't married, but I don't believe that for a moment. Her father would never allow that.

Lastly, is Rowan House. That's where an older lady lives on her own. She's always cooking and makes me wish I could taste, or even smell. Heather is her name. She has a visitor three times a week, like clockwork. Due in about an hour by my reckoning. Quite a dish himself, if you will excuse my little joke."

"You've been very helpful, Elizabeth. If you don't see the light, we have a friend that can help you cross over to repay you."

"I am so looking forward to seeing my ancestors in Heaven. I can't tell you how glad I am that you came. I'm off to find my way." Elizabeth Edenbury bowed her head and went in search of the light.

The three of them walked through the hedge and joined the long cobbled driveway, then up the marble steps to the glass house. "I was right about no one being at home. I can't see anyone there. Ruth must be in Gorebridge. That's a bit of luck."

Abigail wasn't that lucky. They realised that right after they walked through the glass double doors.

"Oh my God. That took ten years off my life," screamed Abigail. "Although, that would make me twenty-nine," she shrugged. The biggest dog they had ever seen had leapt towards them, snarling and growling. "How come he can see us?"

"Animals can have a sixth sense about these things. This must be a guard dog that's trained to attack," said Lillian. "Poor thing, locked up all day. Go away doggie, scoot." The large dog suddenly realised that something was not quite right and ran off howling and whimpering, with his tail between his legs. "I think we know why Leo was killed at the regatta. It would have had to be someone the dog knew if he was killed here."

Abigail said, "Shall we start down here and work our way up? Look, they've got cameras everywhere. I wonder if we'll show up in the videos like we did when we searched Dora Bream's house when she was murdered."

A large area of the downstairs was open-plan with white marble floors. Most of the furniture was white as well. The woodwork, stairs and lamps were black, and there were no photos, except Japanese artwork on the walls. The three of them started to think that the Spencers hadn't got children and weren't thinking of having any. And they must have had some kind of housekeeper, as there was not a speck of dirt or a thing out of place. A huge flower display of pink hydrangeas was on an occasional table by the patio window.

Abigail said, "It doesn't look lived in, does it? Let's try the kitchen. See, not even a mug on the side. Everything neatly in rows as well. I wonder if one of them had a problem. I couldn't live like this. Although, I used to wish my place was tidier."

Lillian added, "Could be that Leo had OCD. Obsessive-compulsive disorder. Seems a bit excessive to kill him for it, though. Might even be her."

"But then again, they might just have a really good cleaner."

"That's true, Suzie."

"Let's find the study. The rich always have a study." It was one of the rooms off the hall and if it was Leo's, he wasn't the one that liked everything in its place. The messy room had a large antique desk, covered in loose papers and a laptop. On the corner there was a pile of brochures featuring his electric bikes. An actual bike and a pile of accessories were in the corner of the room.

"Very nice," said Abigail. "I wish I'd have bought one of these bikes. I'd have done a lot more exercising and got all the way to the top of Chittering Downs. Yes, electric power is definitely my kind of exercise."

Suzie was leafing through the brochure. "And they come in all colours. I love the pink one."

"Whatever next," said Lillian. "It's days like this I'm sorry I'm dead. Can you turn the computer on, Suzie? We might learn how well his business was going. Could be it wasn't doing that well, and he took out a loan from someone he shouldn't have."

"Hmm. Sorry, no I can't. We need his password. I could guess but sometimes you only have three tries and it locks. Mrs

Spencer can give it to the police and then Tom can tell us what's on it."

"No worries, Suzie. What have you found, Abigail?"

"It's his calendar. Look, on Saturday he's written OR, for Ottersmill Regatta I reckon. Then on the Sunday it says, meet NP. Who is NP? Neil, Nancy? There wasn't anyone with the name NP that I can think of. There was a Nina something - Nina Moore though. There was an F, with a phone number, on his desk in the club. Obviously he likes to use initials. Turn it back to January, Suzie. A few other names. Weekends at different bike shows. The Boat Show and a Motorhome Show in April. LN is mentioned once or twice. There's a KIA he mentions quite a bit. It says 'Ask KIA for dates of trials'. In June it says 'Get times off KIA'. Tom will need to find out who she is. Let's try upstairs. If they shared the same bedroom that may give us an idea of what their marriage was like."

It did look like they shared the huge double bedroom that nearly extended over the entire first floor. It led onto a balcony that had a glorious view of the Chiltern Hills. A table and two chairs were out there, and Abigail could imagine how wonderful it would be to sit there in the mornings for coffee and croissants. Sadly that would never happen for her, and now Leo Spencer. She had a sudden feeling of anger at the person who had deprived Leo of his life, and even more fury for the one that had taken her life before she had done all the things she'd had planned. She felt even more unfulfilled when she saw the tiered garden with a kidney-shaped swimming pool. Lillian was looking through their walk-in wardrobe. She sighed and turned round to see that Suzie had opened a drawer of the bedside cabinet and found a diary.

"This belongs to Ruth. There's some names of women. Hair, dentist. She seems to see her doctor quite a bit. Let's get to this weekend. Can't see Rupert Cox anywhere. Just says Regatta. On

Wednesday she has another doctor's appointment. Perhaps she's ill"

"Wow. Perhaps she's not. Look at this, girls," said Abigail. "Lift this up and turn it over for me, Suzie. It says 'Always here for you as a friend and a doctor. Love you' on the back, complete with kisses. Can you read it for us, please, Suzie?"

"Dearest Ruth,

I am so sorry to hear about Leo. Whatever he has done, he did not deserve that. I know that you find it hard to forgive him, but for your sake you need to. We have known each other for years and I have done whatever I can for you. Please don't shut me out now. I took care of your problem before and I can again if you let me, Ruth.

I feel fate brought us together when we bought our houses here when they were built, and didn't realise we would be together again. As for what you told me, we must talk soon. You can't do this alone. I'd do anything for you, and I mean anything.

Always here for you as a friend and a doctor.

Love you. Then there's two kisses."

"Thank you, Suzie. Another suspect then. 'I'd do anything for you.' I wonder if that would mean murder. We'll have to mention it to Tom. Put it back where it was and he'll find it himself soon enough." The four other bedrooms looked like they were for guests, and like the rest of the house, they had that never-used look. I think we should get going before anyone comes." As they went down the stairs they heard voices and the unmistakable bellowing of DCI Johnson at the front door, and saw him through the glass.

"Hurry up, Mrs Spencer, we haven't got all day. Don't forget we don't need a warrant to search the house of a murder victim, so please keep out of our way."

"I know that, Inspector, but I need you to know that…"

"Keep out of my way, please, madam."

"But I was just going to say that you can't just..."

"I won't tell you again, Mrs Spencer. I'll have you arrested. Now let me through."

Abigail, Lillian and Suzie had never laughed so much in all their deaths as Johnson ran down the driveway, chased by Ruth's huge hound, snapping and snarling at the back of his legs. He just managed to jump on the front of a police car and then onto the roof before the dog got to him. Abigail covered Suzie's ears as he shouted to Ruth to get the dog away from him, in his foul-mouthed way. Ruth called "Hector" and he immediately went to her side.

"I'll take him upstairs and put him in our bathroom, Inspector. I did try and warn you," she said with a grin on her face. "What a good boy, Hector. I don't like that nasty man either."

"We finished just in time," said Abigail. "And I wouldn't have missed the look on Johnson's face for the world. I really thought he was going to get a new hole in his old trousers. That was so funny. I've never seen him move that fast."

"Maybe if the pub was about to shut," laughed Lillian.

They left the house for the police to begin their search and saw that Tom had pulled up outside the glass house as they walked away. He had a big grin on his face, so they thought he must have seen the dog chasing his boss. He just wished he had got his phone out a bit quicker to video it.

Abigail stopped suddenly. "That's interesting, can you see what I see at the doctor's house? Pink hydrangeas. Just like the ones in Ruth's display. Our doctor really had it bad. Oh look, the gates are opening. I wonder who that is."

A yellow sports car pulled onto the drive of Rowan House. "That must be the man that visits Heather Lockwood three times a week that Elizabeth told us about. Let's go and see him for ourselves. Oh my. That, my friends, is the gigolo himself - David MacIntosh. And I bet you a bun to a teacake that he's not there to sample her doughnuts."

Chapter 8

THIS TIME DAVID MACINTOSH WASN'T IN LYCRA BUT looked just as hunky, thought Abigail. He was wearing tight black chinos and a slim-fitted grey shirt, with short sleeves that showed off his rower's muscles. Suzie wasn't impressed at all. He was old, she thought. But Lillian quite understood what all the fuss was about now.

Heather had already opened the front door after having buzzed him in the gates. She looked delighted to see him and who wouldn't, thought Abigail. Although, for some silly reason she felt a bit guilty. They might bicker a bit, even a lot, but she did like Terry, although he could be so annoying and grumpy sometimes. And even she had to admit that she could, on occasions, rub someone up the wrong way. Very rarely, of course. And thinking about it, she seemed to remember he was rather taken with a certain Becky Jones who lived in the village and whom he had referred to as Sexy Becksy. She'd remind him of that later.

"Come in, David. Would you like a coffee before we start?"

He gave Heather a kiss on the cheek and put his arm around her as they crossed the spacious hall. "No thank you, darling.

Maybe afterwards. You know how exhausted we both get." Heather was wearing a frilly black and pink dress, more suited to someone in their twenties than their sixties. But Abigail had to admit that she had a good figure, and she hated to think how big her waist would be if she could cook like her. She marvelled at how she was able to pull off the stiletto heels without wobbling like she used to when she wore them.

Abigail turned to Lillian. "Do you think Suzie should stay outside?"

"I'm not going to watch myself! Are you, then?"

"Er, no, of course not. Only in an investigatory way. I wasn't going to be there the whole time, Lillian. We'll stay a bit longer, though, and then have a look around while they, you know."

David had followed Heather into the kitchen where she said, "Do you mind going in and getting everything ready, David? I'm going to do some stretches first. You know what it's like when these old bones start clicking. So be gentle with me, darling."

"Blimey, it's getting worse," giggled Lillian.

"Don't worry, I'll take it slow." David crossed the hall again and went into the lounge. He pushed all the furniture against the far wall, to the bemusement of the three spirits. They could only imagine the activity that was about to occur.

"Coming, ready or not," shouted Heather. They hardly dared to turn round to look, but she still had her clothes on and held a long-stemmed rose between her red lips. She opened a cabinet and started the music.

"Oh," the ghosts said together. "They're dancing. Phew." David and Heather tangoed and foxtrotted for another hour and luckily that was it. They sat on the armchairs and all enjoyed the display. As Suzie said, for a really old woman, she sure could move. Better than she ever could, thought Abigail.

"Will you be staying for cake, David?" asked Heather, as she slipped off her shoes and they went into the kitchen.

"I daresay I could manage a slice or two. Is it your world-famous peach and walnut cake?"

"No. It's a new one I've been doing for the next book. Kiwi and coconut, topped with grated chocolate on butter icing."

"Sounds like another winner. Maybe one slice, as long as you join me, Heather. After the workout we've just had, I think we should allow ourselves a small portion."

"I'll put the kettle on. And don't forget this. And thank you, David. What would I do without you?" A thick envelope was handed to David for his gigolo services. Abigail couldn't help but think that this was possibly his favourite job. He seemed so nice that she was really hoping he didn't turn out to be the killer. But she never had been a good judge of men. Did the two alpha men have a falling out over one of the women at the marina? Maybe Ruth was one of his very long list of clients.

"I suppose you heard about your neighbour."

"Leo? I couldn't believe it, David. Poor Ruth. Have you any idea who did it?"

"Not a clue, literally. It said on the news this morning that he had been hit on the head and thrown in the river. We were all hoping that he had just fallen in. A murder won't do club membership much good. Ben said that Leo had been knocking back the bubbly since he had got there. I mean, I didn't know him that well as I was never on the committee. We would talk about rowing, but that's about it."

"Wasn't it him that hired you as rowing coach?"

"It was more Ruth and Gail Fletcher actually."

Heather laughed. "Hmm, yes, I should imagine they did."

David bristled and shouted, "You may think that, but I'm a bloody good rower, you know. I've got a lot to give the club, Heather. I'm the best instructor that they've ever had. And Oliver and I won all our heats and took the Hatton Challenge Cup yesterday, against the highest competition. I can assure you I wasn't hired for my looks. You're just like the others. They don't think I can do anything else but smile. I thought you were different."

Heather looked like she was going to cry. "I'm so sorry, David. I didn't mean to hurt you. I know you're a fantastic rower and so much more than a handsome face. And I saw your wonderful win yesterday. I popped over for a while yesterday, just to watch you."

"Did you? I'm sorry too. I shouldn't have taken it out on you. But it takes a lot of effort to look this good. Ten years ago, I was a skinny, spotty school kid with no confidence. I've made this happen. I just found I could make more money from women like you than I'd get in an office. You might not believe this, but I have got a brain. I had the chance to go to college, but chose not to. Anyway, let's forget all about it. Tell me about the other recipes in your book."

"So our handsome Adonis has a bad temper," said Abigail. "Enough to kill, I wonder. And Heather was at the regatta as well. I can't wait to get back to the others and tell them what we've seen."

Then Lillian brought up the one question she hadn't thought of till now. How the hell were they going to get back to Becklesfield?!

Chapter 9

AT OTTERSMILL MARINA, A FEW MILES AWAY, HAYLEY had left Terry and Betty to wander about and she made her way to the marina to look at the larger boats that were moored there. Having a boat had never crossed her mind before. Yes, it would be nice to have somewhere to go on a weekend, but they very rarely had free weekends. Not only that, they couldn't afford one of the sailing dinghies, let alone a fancy cruiser. Being a member of the club might be nice, though. It had a nice ring to it; 'We're just going for a drink at our sailing club'.

Hayley had seen two police cars parked nearby, so she knew she had to be careful not to look like she was anything other than a visitor. The biggest boat in the marina was moored nearest the club and it was on that that she saw WPC Jane Nichols. She was thinking of making a quick exit, but Jane spotted her and gave her a wave.

"Hi, Hayley. Tom's not here if you're looking for him. Or are you interested in boats? By the way, don't come aboard this one."

"I was here yesterday at the regatta and thought it might be nice to join the club."

"Not because you want to help with your psychic powers, then?" Jane said sweetly. "It's no secret, you know. Well, it is. But we have guessed and love you for it."

"I'm sure Johnson doesn't agree, Jane. And please try and keep it quiet. Can you imagine if the press got hold of it and knew it was me? Tom's career would be over, and Johnson hates him enough as it is. How's the search going? I see you've got tape over the door. Whose boat is this?"

"It's called a hatch, apparently. An old boy told me. You didn't hear it from me," Jane looked around. "But this belongs to Rupert Cox, the boyfriend, and we found the victim's phone under one of the seats at the back. Forensics and the photographer are on their way, and I'm just waiting for Sergeant Mills to come and take a look."

"Doesn't look good for him, then. Wonder if the merry widow was involved."

"Probably in Johnson's eyes."

"I'd better not be seen talking to you, in case he turns up. He likes me as much as he likes Tom."

"Don't take it personally, Hayley. You know what he's like. So what are your plans now you're here?"

"I'm just going to take a leisurely stroll around and casually ask a few questions. Starting in the shop."

"Chandlery. He told me off for that as well. And by the way, it's not a toilet, it's a head. That I can understand, actually. When I went on a boat across to France, I had my head down one most of the way there. No way would I buy a boat."

"I don't think you'd get seasick on the river, though, Jane," laughed Hayley.

"Don't you believe it. I felt sick when I was down below on this boat, and it's tied up front and back."

"Hilarious, hun. Okay, I'm off to Jack's Chandlery then. Is there a Jack?"

"Yes. That's the bloke that was saying I got the words all wrong. So watch out for that."

"I might be able to use it to my advantage. Some men love to explain things to a stupid woman. I'll let you know. Thanks for the info, Jane. I promise I won't tell a living soul," said Hayley.

The chandlery was a large, converted wooden building that consisted of four rows of shelves and barely room to walk between them. Nearly a whole aisle was taken up with every bolt, nail, and screw that you could possibly imagine. Next to a rack of ropes of every width was a cluttered counter, and sitting behind it was the famous Jack, who was leafing through a sailing magazine.

"What can I do for you, Miss?"

"I'm just looking, thank you. We were at the regatta yesterday and my husband and I thought about getting a boat, so I thought I would just get an idea of prices of things. You know, like the parking."

Jack was horrified, as Hayley was expecting. "Ooh, don't say that. It's mooring, not parking. I'll talk you through it. It's not a cheap hobby for sure. Here's the price list for the mooring fees."

"Oh goodness, that is a bit pricey. Is it extra to be a club member?"

"Not if you have a boat here, then it's included. Were you thinking of a day boat or a cruiser you could sleep on?"

Hayley channelled her inner Betty. "Probably something like a dingey."

"I think you mean a dinghy. Would it be to sail or row? Or even an outboard motor on the back. You need to put a lot of thought into this."

"The motor sounds easier. But then it would be so nice to have a boat with four beds for us and our friends, and a kitchen for having a meal."

"Four berth, they call that. And it's not a kitchen, it's a galley."

The Deadly Regatta

"Well, I certainly would need your help, Jack, is it?"

"That's me. I opened this place thirty years ago. There are a few boats for sale. People buy one when the weather's fine and as soon as the winter comes, they've had enough. I'd give you and your husband a good deal on one."

"Looking at what you sell here, we'd need an awful lot of equipment."

"There's always something going wrong with a boat. They say the best two days when you have a boat are the day you buy it, and the day you sell it. But most of the folks here wouldn't have it any other way. The water is either in your blood, or it's not."

"I heard there was an accident yesterday and that someone had fallen in? But then I overheard a lady saying it might have been murder. It must have happened after we left. Did you hear anything about that?"

"Did I? It was a friend of mine - Leo Spencer. I've known him for many years. Ever since he used to come with his parents and learnt how to row and sail. He was a local lad. Must have been an outsider. No one I know would have killed him. I still think it's an accident. He liked a drink or two, as do most of the boaters. Me included."

"It must be some maniac, Jack. I feel so sorry for his family. Was he married?"

"He was. His wife, Ruth, is the treasurer. And she is a treasure too. Whatever they're saying about her cheating on him. A beautiful woman, inside and out. I see the police are searching her friend Rupert's boat today. Nice craft. Bit too big for here though. He used to moor it at Henley, so I don't know what he'd want to come here for."

"Must be cheaper fees, I suppose. Between you and me, Jack, I heard the murder weapon was an anchor thingy."

"No, who told you that? I'll show you exactly what killed

him, because the sergeant came in yesterday asking if I had sold any lately. Come with me."

Jack got off his stool and led her to the far wall, where the anchors were kept and picked up what would have indeed been a lethal weapon in deadly hands.

"What on earth is that, Jack? That's not an anchor like the ones I've seen. Where does that go on a boat?"

"You've done your motoring upstream for the day and you want to stop, but there are no rings to tie to, or posts available. You'd hammer one of these in the bank and thread your rope through this link. Most people call them mooring pins or stakes. If you've got a larger boat, you'd need two."

"Front and back?"

"Bow and stern, yes. Else you'd swing round with the current."

Hayley picked one up and moved it from side to side. "It looks pretty lethal. And quite a weight. And had you sold one recently?"

"I probably shouldn't say, but I have sold a couple in the last month. One was for cash, so I haven't got a record of that, and I can't for the life of me remember who to. But funnily enough, the other one was to Rupert Cox."

"No. It must be him then."

"Be a bit daft to use that after paying for it on a credit card. But I guess he must have lost his temper. Word is he likes Mrs Spencer, so who knows. I'm hoping it was some nutter or an accident. Won't be good for business if there's a murderer running about."

"Might even increase trade. Some people on the internet like that kind of thing."

"I've got no time for that Facetok or anything like that."

"It's free publicity for a start, and then people soon forget. I'd better get going. You've been so kind, Jack. Thank you so much. May I take a copy of the prices? I'll show my husband.

Could be I just have some sailing lessons to start with. A friend of mine takes them with David something."

"David MacIntosh. Are you sure it's sailing? He gives all sorts of lessons. If I were you, I'd steer clear of him. Use Nina Moore. She teaches the young nippers."

"Okay, well thank you. Is the club open for a drink? Can I get in without membership?"

"Yes. Barry will take anyone's money. Come back soon. I'm here every day - eight till four. And watch out for that David. He's a good-for-nothing."

Hayley agreed, but there were a large number of women in the Chiltern Hills area who thought he was very good for something.

She didn't leave there until she made sure that no other policemen were wandering about. It was all quiet so she slipped into the bar and luckily there were none in there either. There were a lot more people in there than she would have imagined on a Monday lunchtime. It seemed boats and booze went together for most of them. Hayley felt out of place with her flowing long skirt and flat, strappy sandals. Everyone else was wearing trousers and deck shoes. Barry, who she had been told about, was behind the bar, and Moira was collecting glasses and wiping the tables down with a grey cloth. By the look on her face, the woman in her thirties did not think she would be doing this when she had married the slightly older Barry.

Hayley made a beeline for the empty table to strike up a conversation with her. "Excuse me, will it be alright to get a drink?"

"No problem. Come up to the bar. What can I get you?"

Hayley would have preferred to have water, but looking around that would look a bit suspicious. "Gin and tonic, please. No ice. I was here for the regatta and now I'm checking the place out properly. I'm starting to love it. Have you worked here long?"

"Too long. Me and my husband run the bar and live upstairs. About six years now. We're both from the next village born and bred - Tingleford."

Barry moved to the other end of the bar to serve two elderly couples, who looked like they had spent their whole lives sailing and boating. It was a good chance to have a proper talk with the wife that Tom had been told liked a good gossip.

"So you moved from that village to here. Are you worried that you haven't seen much of the big world yet?"

Moira shrugged. "I have, unlike misery guts down there. Believe it or not, I'm slightly overqualified to pull pints and wash tables and floors. I went to university and took a business degree. What happened? Barry did, I guess. Love has a lot to answer for. I could kick myself now, of course. My mum and dad tried to warn me, but did I listen to them? Obviously not," she said, as she gave Hayley her drink and wiped down the mahogany bar. "I've had enough. I thought I'd be living in our own home with six kids by now."

"So, what do you do for fun? Sailing or boating?"

"Good Lord, no. I used to row at uni, but not anymore. I have my fun wherever I can these days. Watch this." Moira shouted over to a bearded man in a hoodie. "Roger, was that your Anita I saw getting on Rory's boat? It's a wonder you put up with that. Mind you, she's a good-looking woman."

"I trust her."

"Yeah, but do you trust Rory?" Moira went back to Hayley. "I like to know what's going on and mix it up a little. I'd die of boredom otherwise. You'd be surprised what I overhear, or eavesdrop on, it's all the same to me. Like with this murder, I'm going to work out who did it. I love all the detective books and shows. Columbo and all that. I record them all so I can watch when I'm not stuck in here. I know just how to do it. Let them do all the talking while I just listen. They always say something incriminating in the end if you just keep your mouth shut." That's what I'm doing now, thought Hayley.

"And who have you got in mind as the murderer so far? It was the commodore that was killed, wasn't it?"

"That's right, Leo. I see it all in here. I could name three or four suspects already, but I won't. Why should I help that awful Johnson man? I'd rather just show him up at the end. But, Mrs Leo was knocking off one of the boat owners. And the dead man was seeing someone himself?"

"Leo was? Really. Who was that then?"

Moira checked that her husband wasn't near enough to hear and then said, "I've been told by the police not to discuss things, so you could torture me and I wouldn't tell you that Leo Spencer had been meeting up with Nina Moore for the last year. They both come from around here. There she is over there. Looks like butter wouldn't melt in her mouth, doesn't it? Much younger than him as well. Why are you so interested? Not a journalist, are you? There's been loads of them in here. Or worse still, an undercover cop. We've answered enough questions."

Hayley decided to be honest with her. "Definitely not. I won't tell a living soul anything you say. I'm actually a psychic medium and felt drawn to come here today."

"To speak to me?" asked Moira, looking worried.

"No, not at all. I felt like I needed to come and make sure that the victim's spirit was not here still. But he's not. I don't sense he's here at all. But one thing I want to say to you, is be careful. This murderer has already killed once. Suppose the killer overheard you say you were going to find him or her. Or you might get close and end up in the river yourself. Watch what you say, and watch what you do, please. You're playing a very dangerous game. Leave it to the police." Hayley couldn't help but feel very hypocritical giving Moira this advice. She was doing the exact same thing. But she tried to keep it quiet and she wasn't daft enough to tell a bar full of suspects like Moira just had. Hayley knocked back her drink as she noticed Nina was leaving, and she was hoping to be able to chat with her, and bring up the subject of sailing lessons. Especially after she found out that she was going out with Leo. Ottersmill Marina was turning out to be a very small community. After the warning she had given to Moira, she decided to be careful from now on. For all she knew, old Jack could be the murderer and she had just shown an unhealthy interest in who had killed Leo. It was the same with Nina; it could easily be her. Betty would definitely remark about a woman scorned or something like that.

Nina seemed in a hurry and Hayley thought she wouldn't be able to catch her up. She turned left at the riverbank, or downstream, Jack would have corrected her, and didn't slow down until she reached a small, dilapidated motor cruiser, and went below into the small cabin. Hayley felt the young girl's pain as the sound of sobbing filled the air. Here at least was someone that would miss poor Leo Spencer. Not one person that she knew of had wept for him. Maybe his wife had when she got home last night, but there were only a few tears when she was first told of his violent death. It could have been shock, but if anyone had told her that about Tom, Hayley had a feeling that she wouldn't be able to stop crying. Hayley decided to put aside any thoughts of questioning Nina and to just give her some comfort. This girl was hurting. This girl needed Hayley Moon and her empathy, not Hayley Bennett, even if she was a murderer or was told to go away.

"Hello, Nina. Could I have a word, hun?"

"Who is it?" she answered, sniffing. A pretty face with red eyes and wet cheeks appeared through the hatch.

"My name is Hayley. I heard you crying and wondered if I could help. I'm an empath and a psychic medium."

"I haven't got any money."

Hayley could never work out why they always said that straight off. Nothing was ever further from her thoughts.

"Oh goodness, I don't want any money for what I do. I swear."

"Okay. Give me a moment and I'll get us a lemonade and we can sit on the back. I could do with someone to talk to. I feel like I'm going mad." Hayley had the ability to get strangers to confide in her. It was one of the many gifts that Tom loved her for.

"I'm not prying, I saw you in the bar and I felt an intense sadness around you, and so I followed you. I hope you don't mind."

"I feel so alone, Hayley, did you say? This is my parents' boat but they don't come anymore. We used to have a sailing boat on the coast in Essex and went every weekend. It was lovely there. We'd go up the coast and back. That's where I got my sailing qualifications. But the journey took longer and longer on the Friday and the weather got worse. A squall would appear out of nowhere and that was enough for Mum to sell the boat. Global warming more than likely. So we came here, but it's not the same as being out at sea."

"Is that when you started seeing him?"

Nina looked surprised. "Leo? I bet Moira told you. I hate her. How much do you know?"

"I know you loved Leo and now he's gone, and you can't openly grieve for him. I know you're worried that the police will find out and think you had something to do with it. And worse of all, you're worried about what his wife will do or say. But I'm also sensing something else. Anger? Resentment? Did Leo break it off?"

"How did you know that? Oh my God, the police are going to think I had a reason to kill him now. He rang me on the first day of the regatta, on Saturday morning, to say it was over. I was absolutely furious. I wanted to meet up to talk about it but he said no, there was no point, it was over and there was nothing to talk about. But I had to know why, so I kept ringing but he didn't answer. I sent him all sorts of texts. God, some of them will sound like threats now. Let's hope his mobile's at the bottom of the river. But I've heard you can put it in rice and it dries it out. I've had it." Nina started to cry again.

Hayley didn't like to tell her that it had just been found on Rupert Cox's boat. Johnson would be over the moon to have a third suspect.

"If I was you, hun, I'd ring up the Gorebridge Police Station and ask for Sergeant Dave Mills. He's very nice and will help you through it. I probably shouldn't say, but my husband is a constable, so I might be able to tell him. But it would be much better if it came from you. You'd look far less guilty. Or there's WPC Nichols over by the marina. You could have a word with her. I could introduce you."

"Thank you so much. I feel a bit better already. I hardly had any sleep last night."

"For what it's worth, I can only feel your sadness and no guilt. Have you got any idea why he finished with you?"

"The only thing he said was that he'd seen something that had changed everything. He didn't say what. He was fine in the club on Thursday night, so whatever it was happened on Friday, or Saturday morning before ten o'clock. That was when he came and told me. I was devastated."

"And he said he'd seen something, not heard something?" asked Hayley.

"Definitely seen something. So it was after he left me on Thursday. Or even when he got here first thing on the Saturday. He wouldn't tell me. Oh Hayley, do you think whatever he saw was what got him killed?"

"Perhaps. And if that's the case, it was a good job he didn't tell you. You might have been next."

"Please could you help me? I know you're not the police or

anything, but I need to know. Could you find out who did it? Ask around the marina perhaps. I can't pay you or anything."

"Our meeting must be fate, because I've been thinking of putting a kind of detective agency on my website to help people, and you could be our first client. It's just me and a few friends, but I can honestly say it will be totally confidential, they won't tell anyone. Don't worry about the cost. We'll take a few free cases to get us going. First thing I need to know is have you got an alibi for Leo's murder? He was attacked roughly between two and half past three."

"If that's true, then I have, thank goodness. I was with the Nippers. The last race of the day is a fun raft race for the children and I was sorting that out as well. So there's loads of kids and parents that can vouch for me."

"Well, there you go. I bet you feel a lot better now. Did you see Leo at all yesterday? The police will need to know his movements and yours on the day."

"I went into one of the marquees to get something to eat, but he was with her, so I left."

"Did he look happy or worried?"

"That was the thing, he looked happy. But he always enjoyed the regatta and I suppose they had to put on a good show as they're both on the committee. And I couldn't say a word, so I tried to convince myself that it was over. She's so beautiful as well. I never did know what he saw in me."

"Youth, kindness and innocence, I think, Nina. I have a feeling you will meet someone soon that will be far more suitable. Not David MacIntosh though."

"Don't worry, I'm not his type. I was hoping at one point because he's so gorgeous, but I gave up on him ages ago. He wasn't interested in me at all. Between you and me, I wonder if he's gay?"

Hayley stifled a laugh. "No, that's not it, hun, believe me.

Looks aren't everything, don't forget. Although they go a long way with him."

"I know. Even my mum likes him."

"I see someone that loves sailing, and not rowing, in your future. I don't think you've met him yet. Look out for a young man with the initials S and K. What exactly do you do here?"

"I teach the cadets how to sail on a Wednesday afternoon and Sunday morning. This is one of the few places where the river is wide enough. Being the commodore, Leo would often come to watch."

"How old are you?"

"Twenty-four"

"Really? You're only a few years younger than me but you look a lot younger."

"Everyone says that. I think that was part of the charm for Leo. He used to call me his Little Ninny." Nina's voice broke and Hayley felt a wave of sympathy for her. "I was LN on his phone, thinking about it. So they might not know it's me. But they'll have my number, won't they? The age gap never bothered me. He was so much more exciting than men my age. We could go out in his convertible to high-class restaurants and a couple of times we even went to the theatre in London and stayed the night in a five-star hotel. A totally different life for me. I'm not even sure if these tears are for me or for Leo. He was my life. I thought of nothing else from the time I woke up till I went to sleep."

"Do you work as well or is it just the sailing?"

"I'm a teaching assistant at Tingleford Primary. I went there myself and I love kids. I suppose if the affair gets in the paper I might get fired. And lose giving the sailing lessons when it all comes out. Everyone will hate me for hurting poor Ruth."

"Not necessarily. You're a great tutor and the children would miss you. And don't worry about Ruth. She's not the angel you think she is, and it seems that most people know that. Yours isn't the only love triangle to come out. And you know what shape two triangles put together make?"

"Er, a square?" answered Nina.

"Nope. It all comes out pear-shaped. Believe me."

"I had heard a few things about Ruth and one of the boat owners, but Leo refused to hear anything bad said about her. Which I always thought was strange. It was almost like he felt sorry for her, but he would never tell me why."

"I have a feeling there's a lot more to come out about their relationship. And strictly between us, DCI Johnson has already got a pretty good suspect. And I have a friend called Abigail who is brilliant at working out clues, if he gets it wrong. Take my card, it's got my name and website. Let me write the number of the police station on it. And don't forget, ask for Sergeant Mills and whatever you do, don't speak to DCI Johnson. He's in charge but he's not nice. It's probably best not to mention to anyone there that you've spoken to me. But don't worry, Nina, me and my friends will make sure you will be alright. In fact, I need to go and find two of them. They're wandering around somewhere investigating, blending into the background, almost like they're invisible!"

Chapter 10

Terry had been hoping he could have spent the day at the marina with Abigail instead of with Betty. They had even talked about their dream date once, and that included a boat on the river, followed by a picnic. Although Terry in reality would not have liked that at all, mainly due to the fact that he couldn't swim. He couldn't tell Abigail that, especially after all the comments about that rower bloke from all the ladies. Would he just sink to the bottom now? He didn't feel the need to try. However, he and Betty were enjoying sitting on a bench, watching the boats go by. It was still busy, even if it was a Monday. It was nearly the end of the children's school holidays and who knew how many days of summer were left for going up and down the river. He realised Betty had been talking and had to admit that he hadn't been listening.

"I was asking if you saw the man sitting on the upturned boat. He was a Dead, of course. We'll go and ask him if he knows anything presently."

"I didn't notice him. Are you sure he was dead?"

"Definitely, Terry. I'm getting good at telling the difference. You must have seen him. He had a tweed jacket and one of those flat caps. You know, like in that programme. What was it now? My son and John used to love it. It was set in Birmingham in the nineteen-thirties. It was, I know, The Sneaky Peakies."

"Never heard of it. Was it a kiddy thing? Sounds like it."

"I'm not sure. I didn't really watch it. Anyway, he looked like one of them. So he could have been here for years. There are worse places, I suppose."

"Absolutely, Betty. I'm going to try and get Abigail to come here with me. It's funny, she rubs me up the wrong way half the time, and the other half I rather like her."

"I'd say it was a bit more than that. She likes you too, I'm sure. She can be a bit of a know-it-all. But then, to be honest, she does know it all."

"You've hit the nail on the head there, Betty."

"I know. The trouble is, she knows she's a know-it-all because she does know it all and likes it when everyone else knows it."

"I know," said Terry with a laugh. "As I say, love and hate. Come on. We'd better get a move on because we know nothing and we don't want Abigail to know it."

"Don't I know it. And we don't even know where to start. Let's see if we can find the Sneaky Peaky man."

"Hayley can do the shop and the clubhouse. We could go to the offices and see if we can learn anything in the places where she can't get into."

"Good idea, Terry. If we don't learn anything, Abi will have our guts for gutters."

"I couldn't have put it better myself," fibbed Terry. "Is that him over there? The Peaky Sneaky man?"

Betty tutted. "The Sneaky Peakies. I'll have to get Suzie to put it on in the library one night. It's about a family after the Great War, so we'll all enjoy it. Good wholesome fun, and a good history lesson for Suzie. It'll take our minds off all the murders and violence as well. Excuse me, sir. Could we have a little chat? This is Terry Styles and I'm Betty. Pleased to meet you."

"Willy Morgan. Nice to meet you both. Are you new?"

"It's been a couple of years for me, but Terry died about fifty years ago."

Terry shook his hand. "I reckon you died about the time I was born, late thirties?"

"Early forties. Missed the war. I could only watch. I don't know what happened to my family. But I'm happy here for the best part. What brings you two here?"

"Murder most foul," said Betty dramatically. "The one yesterday. I don't suppose you saw anything, did you, Willy?"

"'Fraid not. The first I knew of it was when all the police came. I saw him though."

"Who? The murderer?"

"No. The poor bugger that got his head bashed in."

Terry and Betty both spoke together. "He's still here?"

"He was just after. He didn't have a clue what had happened."

"Did he say anything?" asked Terry.

"He didn't say who did it, if that's what you're wondering. All he said was, 'It's mine'. He never said what was. Then I heard a whoosh and he ran into the light. I'm not sure he even meant to. But he was gone, nevertheless. Obviously I didn't know he'd been murdered. Just assumed he'd fallen in like the others before him. And I didn't see anyone that looked like they could've done it. Murder; that's a first for here. Plenty of deaths though. Mine for a start. I keeled over, pardon my little joke, when I was working on my hull. I've had eighty years to make that up," he laughed. "Most of them go by drowning. Most of them are caused by drinking."

"They say don't drink and drive," said Betty. "But I suppose a boat is as lethal as a car after a few glasses of whisky."

"What I'd give for a drop of whisky at this minute. I still

miss it after all this time. And a cigarette," Willy said sadly. "I must have smoked too much because when I get close to the living they always say, 'Can you smell cigarette smoke?' Wish I could."

"Our friend says she can smell my perfume."

"You've got a real live friend?"

Terry said, "Yes. We're lucky like that. Her name is Hayley. She's one of those mediums if you've heard of them."

Willy stroked his beard. "I've heard of them, but never met one. I used to wish I had. There was so much unsaid when I died. To my wife and kids, I wanted to say I could have been there more and down the pub less. They're all gone now. Great-great-grandkids about maybe, but they won't know my name."

"Why don't you move on, Willy?"

"I've thought about it. Scared of what I'll find out and where I'll go, I suppose. One day."

"I don't suppose you know a young man called David. He caught our eye when he was bending over getting his oars out of his boat thingies."

"Rowlocks," said Willy.

"No, it's true, isn't it, Terry?"

Willy roared with laughter. "Ah, Betty, you're so funny. I like a woman with a sense of humour. If you ever fancy a change of scene you're welcome to join me here. We can have a pick of whatever boat is going out and have a grand time."

"I suppose I could. I don't think my John would mind. I'll let you know. But if you did want to pass over, our friend, Hayley, can help. She knows everything about it," said Betty. "You're in luck, here she is." But the old man had disappeared at the thought of someone who could send him to an unknown fate.

"Well, I learned a lot. How about you two? Can I smell cigarettes?" said Hayley, crinkling up her nose.

"Yes, it was a local chap called Willy Morgan. You've just missed him. A dear old soul," said Betty.

"You scared him off, but he was rather smitten with Betty."

"Oh, Betty, you've still got it then."

"There's life in the old dog yet, as they say. But forget about my sex life with Willy for a minute," which tickled Hayley. "Willy said he saw Leo after the murder and heard a whoosh as he went into the light. And the only thing he said was, 'It's mine'."

"That's interesting. We might need to find out the where and when from him. Perhaps you and Abi could come back here for a date and ask him."

"That did cross my mind, actually. Hmm, I'll ask her. What say we go back to the library and see if the others are back from Leo's house? Then I can mention it."

"Good idea," said Hayley. "Let's see if we can get to the car before someone catches me and tells Tom or Johnson. I've got so much to tell you that I promised I wouldn't tell to a living soul!"

Luckily for Abigail, Lillian and Suzie, Hayley's red Mini pulled over when they still had two miles to walk back to Becklesfield.

Hayley lowered the window and shouted, "Hop in. That's good timing, it's going to rain soon." She reached over to open the door but they were already in, by going through it. She often forgot they were all dead and felt even sillier when she asked if they had put their seatbelts on. Hayley felt quite proud of herself when the rain she predicted began as soon as she pulled away. And Terry was more than happy as well when Abigail sat on his lap in the crowded car.

They arrived at her house in Church Lane, the one with the wind chimes and dreamcatcher, and sat there until the rain eased. They swapped what they had all learned and all was going well until Abigail learned what Willy Morgan had told Terry and Betty.

"So Leo said 'It's mine', just after he died. But did he say it in a creepy Lord of the Rings way? Or was it a 'get off' way? Or

'I'm so happy it's mine' way? Or even an 'okay I give up, it's mine' way?"

Terry and Betty looked downcast. "Oh, sorry, Abi, we never thought to ask, did we?" said Betty. "But look, that means you and Terry will have to go back to the river and ask him, looking on the bright side."

"Good idea. And sorry, I wasn't having a go. We often don't think of these things at the time. It's no problem."

Feeling better, they all arranged to meet the next morning at the Becklesfield Public Library, where they all had no doubt that Abigail would tell them exactly what they were going to do next.

Hayley was just going to open her front door when she had a phone call from an unknown number. It was Suzie's mother, Sonia. She was answering Hayley's text asking if they could meet at some point. Hayley knew how busy she was going to be for the next few days with the case, and so she suggested she could drive to Little Chortle, where Sonia lived and meet at their village pub. A meeting was arranged and Hayley reversed the car out of her drive. She hoped Suzie was still on her way back to the library, as there was no point going without her. Luckily, her friends had only got as far as the village green and so Suzie excitedly got in the car with Hayley, to give Sonia a psychic reading that she would never forget.

Sonia walked the five minutes to the Three Horseshoes and ordered herself a white wine. She thought that she might need it. The text had simply said that this lady was a psychic medium called Hayley, who had been in contact with Suzie. And not to worry as she did not want any money. Part of her did worry that it might be a con, but she so wanted to believe that she had taken the chance and arranged to meet her. Sonia had written a list of questions to ask, or rather to test this Hayley. She took her white wine and sat at a table in the garden area of the three-hundred-year-old coaching inn. The seats were a bit wet from the earlier shower, but she didn't want to be in an enclosed space with this woman. That must be her, she thought. A lady with long black hair, flowing clothes and beads around her neck had walked out of the pub into the garden, holding a drink. A witch in a past life, was Sonia's first thought.

Hayley saw the only black woman and knew it must be her. But Suzie had already run over there to put her arms around her. Sonia felt a cold breeze envelop her as she had done many times before, and prayed that this was the spirit of her beautiful daughter. She was about to find out if it had been just her imagination in the past.

Hayley put down her glass. "Sonia? I'm Hayley. How are you?"

"I'm fine. A bit nervous to be honest. I'm not sure if I'm a true believer."

"I expect you've got a few questions to ask first. But before you do, can I say that Suzie is sitting next to you on the bench and she looks so pretty in her flowery dress. And she's got the biggest smile on her face."

Suzie touched her hand and Sonia flinched. "I do believe, but I'm worried that it's just wishful thinking. Can I ask you a few things that only my daughter would know?"

"Of course, fire away."

Sonia took out her list that she had thought long and hard about. "The first question is, what did her daddy call her when she was younger?"

"Suzie says Pumpkin."

"That's right. What did I call her?"

"Dumpling. And she's saying there seems to be a bit of a pattern. She says was she chunky?"

Sonia laughed. "No, she was perfect. She still has her funny sense of humour then. But sorry, Hayley, you could be guessing or psychic, but I need to know she is really here. This will be the last one, I promise. What colour was her blankie?"

"It was lilac, with a rainbow in the corner, which was hanging off." Sonia pressed her lips together to stop herself from crying.

"Suzie is telling me that Jordan had a hamster called Fang, which he never wanted to clean out. And when it died he put it in the airing cupboard in case it was just hibernating."

As Hayley was relaying this, Sonia grabbed both of her hands. "Thank you. Thank you so much. My baby is here. I need to ask her, was she in pain when she died?"

"No. She said she didn't feel any pain. Only the pain of seeing you suffer. She knows you never left her side until she passed away, and then you only let go of her hand when they made you. And when you kissed her head you said, 'It's not goodbye, it's till we meet again'."

"I did. I'd forgotten I said that. Why hasn't she gone to Heaven with Jesus?"

"Suzie is telling me, she's waiting for you. Don't worry about her. She is happy and has a lot of friends. She wants me to tell you about Lillian Yin."

"Who is Lillian?" asked Sonia.

"Lillian was a nurse in life and was at the hospital when Suzie was brought into the emergency room. She had died there herself and felt drawn to her because she worked with sick children. You didn't know, Sonia, but Lillian told you that she would look after her until you came. She absolutely dotes on her, and she didn't come today so you can have her all to yourself."

"Please thank her for me. But you should move on, Suzie. We can still meet up on the other side however long it takes."

"Suzie really doesn't want to. Also she wants to be there for Jordan. That's the only negative thing that we have to tell you, Sonia."

"My son? What's the matter with Jordan?"

"We know that you think that he took his sister's death very badly, and he did. But he is starting to heal. But what Suzie and Lillian found out was that he was being bullied by some other boys. They took care of it, by scaring the leader half to death, but Jordan needs to talk to you about it."

"I had no idea. Why on earth didn't he tell me?"

"I think because it wouldn't have helped at school, but also he feels like he has to be the strong one for you. He knows you can't bring yourself to talk about Suzie with him, in case it upsets him, but he wants to. It's none of my business, but you both need to lift each other. Maybe it's time to stop grieving and look back on what a happy life Suzie had before the accident. Laugh about the fun times, remember her sense of humour and even talk about the sad times. Suzie is saying that whenever she comes home, Jordan is upstairs in his room and you are downstairs. It breaks her heart."

"We need to talk, I know. I don't want to lose Jordan as well. I wonder if I should tell him about today."

Hayley frowned. "It's up to you. But personally, I wouldn't. He's fourteen, isn't he? Teenagers have it hard enough as it is. You don't want him thinking he would like to join her, if you know what I mean."

"I do, Hayley, and the thought has gone through my head a lot. I worry about him all the time. You're right. Maybe when he's older. I need to spend more time thinking of Jordan and less on Suzie. If that's alright with her?"

Suzie kissed her mummy's cheek and said, "Please enjoy your lives. I would get so much joy if I could see you both happy again. I'm happy, Mummy, and one day we'll be together. Like you said, it was never goodbye, just till we meet again."

Hayley's voice broke as she told Sonia, and it took all her strength to not break down completely. "How wonderful that she heard me say that."

"Hayley, tell Mummy it's Jordan's first day back at school tomorrow and I'm going to be there to see he's alright. So she needn't worry about him."

"I'm so pleased, Suzie," Sonia answered. "I don't know if you realise this, but it would have been your first day at secondary school tomorrow, darling."

Suzie blinked hard. "I didn't know. I'd forgotten and that breaks my heart, but don't tell her I'm upset, please, Hayley."

"Suzie said she is fine with that. And in a way she will be going. Just in another realm. And she knows Jordan is the important one. She is such a credit to you, Sonia. She's the kindest child I've ever met. I'll let you know what happens with Jordan, if that is alright?"

"I'll watch him, Mummy. Nobody is ever going to hurt my brother again."

The next day at Chortle Academy, Suzie kept her promise, but faced a challenge far greater than she thought she would.

Chapter 11

HAYLEY FELT PHYSICALLY AND MENTALLY EXHAUSTED by the time she got home from talking to Sonia. But she also felt very proud of herself. It had all gone well and Sonia had been so nice. Occasionally the families got very angry with her for talking about their loved ones. They either called her a liar, or even worse once, a criminal. But that was the burden she had to bear. She knew that, and she wouldn't have given up her gift for the world. But it did take it out of her and she just needed to rest for a while.

She was so looking forward to Tom getting home from his shift, and he could give her a big hug. Of course, Luna, her rescue cat, assumed she was there purely for his needs, and didn't let Hayley do any resting or anything else until he had been fed, played with and generally spoiled for at least an hour. Only then could Hayley sit on the sofa and write down all that they had learned about the case. If she was going to write a book about their cases she needed to keep notes. While she had some time to spare she added the advert for the agency to her psychic website.

> NOW AVAILABLE
> THE DEADLY DETECTIVE AGENCY
> ANY PROBLEMS GREAT OR SMALL
> NATURAL OR SUPERNATURAL
> USE OUR EXCELLENT DETECTIVE SERVICES
> ALL CASES DEALT WITH IN CONFIDENCE
> COMPETITIVE RATES

Her finger hovered over the PUBLISH button for a few seconds, but she closed her eyes and went for it. What could possibly happen? No one would see it anyway. Perplexingly, another feeling came over her. She had no choice in the matter. Hayley knew she had to put the advert somewhere else. She added her email address and her mobile number, and then she looked up the website for the Chiltern Weekly, personal advertisements section. There was someone out there that needed their help, she was sure of it. Hayley had to wonder if it was to do with the picture of the little girl that still haunted her dreams. She really hoped not, and she had a feeling that it was something far more deadly.

By the time Hayley had had a bit of a nap and done all her jobs, Luna was awake again and expected his required VIP treatment. That was until Tom got home, whereupon he totally ignored Hayley and spent all his time with him, even though Tom hadn't even wanted to keep the 'damn cat'. But now he couldn't imagine life without him and loved him like a baby. Luna never left Tom's side, even during the night. Sometimes it wasn't even by his side, it was more on top.

They had a lovely dinner of tuna pasta, and didn't talk about murders or murderers, which was so nice. But as they drank their coffee they began to swap information on the case. The first thing Hayley wanted to know was what Johnson had made of the love letter to Ruth from Doctor Sharma who lived next door.

Tom looked puzzled. "What letter is that? We didn't find a letter from a doctor. Where was it?"

"Abigail said it was on the dressing table in the main bedroom. They left it where it was, I'm sure."

"Then she must have moved it when she took the dog upstairs. That was so funny by the way. I got there just in time to see Johnson running for his life and leaping on his car. I wouldn't have thought he could run that fast."

"It made the girls' day as well. Ruth did try to warn him apparently."

"He never listens to anyone, as you know. So what was in the letter?"

"Not sure I know myself properly. Something about I've always been there for you after what you went through. I will be again, especially now. Then love and kisses from your doctor and friend. And Abigail noticed there was a fresh flower display in Ruth's lounge that matched the flowers in his front garden."

"I'll have to tell Dave about the letter and he can make something up for the boss." They were both close to Sergeant Mills and his wife, Isabella. Mills knew the information was coming from Tom's psychic wife and was quite happy to get credit for any ideas. What he didn't know was there was an agency on hand that then passed the details to Hayley.

Tom went on, "And the autopsy results came back. Nothing that we hadn't already guessed. I know I shouldn't, but I took a photo of it. Listen. Leo Spencer – aged 42. Time of death – two to four pm. Umm, no water in lungs, so death was instantaneous. Otherwise healthy. Where does it say about the weapon? Right. Steel Ground Anchor. Length 61cm. Diameter 20mm. Weight 1.7kg. Possibly killed by a left-handed assailant. No fingerprints or DNA."

"We all checked and not one of the people we spoke to today was left-handed," Hayley said.

The Deadly Regatta

"The only one so far is Rupert, isn't it? Did you hear the phone was found on his boat by Jane?"

"Yes. I had a word with her just after she'd found it. It was on the deck though, so anyone could have lifted the seat and dropped it in."

"The uniforms will have to go back and talk to everyone that was there to see if they saw anyone going on board."

Hayley pursed her lips together. "But it could have been put there anytime. After Rupert became a suspect, he or she might have decided to put the phone there. Could have been late last night or this morning."

"You're getting good at this, darling."

"I know, hun. Abigail must be rubbing off on me. What happened to Rupert and Ruth today? Were they officially questioned?"

"Not yet. They both came in with what they were wearing and gave their statements and signed them. Rupert was free to go, but Ruth had to be there while they searched the house. They don't need a warrant for a victim's house. They asked permission to search Rupert's boat and he gave it. So why would he have left the phone there, with all that water about? He won't be so keen for them to search his house, so they will need a warrant. I wonder if his wife knows all about his affair."

"I bet she does now, poor woman. Has Ruth got a boat? They must have if he's the commodore."

"No, they haven't. Because Leo went to Oxford and rowed for them, he got the job on that. And he grew up near there. Since he's been in charge they've gone right up in the rowing tables."

"I see. Did they have any luck on working out what was on Leo's calendar? He seemed to have a lot of business trips for boat and caravan shows and I think there was a Kia and he wrote NP on the day of the regatta."

"Not yet. Early days though. His wife gave us the password

for his computer, but there wasn't much to help us. It was mostly for his cycling business. Looks like there's a lot of money in electric bikes. Same as with cars, I guess. They'll keep looking though."

Hayley blew out her cheeks. "Now I've got a bit of information for you, but I can't tell you everything because I promised I wouldn't. There's another person that you need to speak to. Did anyone phone up this afternoon and ask to speak to Dave?"

"Not that he told me. Who is it?"

"A girl called Nina Moore. She teaches sailing in the Nippers Club. She was having an affair with Leo."

"For God's sake, Hayley, you can't keep that to yourself."

"I know, hun. That's why I told her to ring the station. But she didn't kill him. She's got an alibi, I promise."

"So she says. Murderers always do, till you find out that they haven't. If she didn't ring you'll have to come in and make a statement."

"Really? Not to Johnson though. But I'm sure she will have, I hope. Unless she made a slow getaway on that old boat. It's a bit late to text Dave, so make sure you let me know tomorrow."

"Is there anything else you haven't shared, Hayley?"

"Oh, we're getting a boat. Well, we're not now. I've seen how much they cost. And it's an arm and a leg to put them somewhere, so forget it. The only other thing we learned is that we met an old man who heard a whoosh and saw Leo go into the light. And his last words were 'It's mine'. But we've no idea what. So he might have been arguing with someone. I don't think you can use that in a court of law though."

"No, but it is amazing. And that's the kind of investigating I like to hear from you. That can't get you in any trouble or danger. So what was his name? Do you know where he lives?"

"His name is Willy Morgan. But he doesn't actually live anywhere, if you get my meaning."

"Oh, I see. I thought that it was funny that I hadn't heard

anything about a witness. Silly me. You think I'd know better by now. So I'll have to leave him to you, I guess."

"Oh yes, there was one more thing that you should know. I spoke to Moira, the lady behind the bar and she reckons she's a budding sleuth because of all the whodunits she watches. And she says she's going to be the one that catches the killer. I told her that could put her in danger."

"Another one who thinks she's Miss Marple. That's all we need."

"I think she's bored, but she does seem to know what goes on around there. It was her that told me about Nina Moore or else we might not have known. Oh, I forgot, there will be a lot of calls and texts from Nina on Leo's phone when the tech guys take a look. Under LN - Little Ninny, apparently. I think there might have been an LN on the calendar. But that's all I'm saying. And don't tell them about LN because she told me that in confidence, I just remembered. And don't tell me off, but I told Nina we would take her on as our first client on the DDA to make sure she doesn't get arrested."

"Hayley, you're getting far too involved. She could be the murderer for all you know."

"I know she's not. I would know… I think."

"Well, be careful for God's sake. And keep out of Johnson's way."

"Before you get too mad, don't forget you wouldn't have known about that love letter if it hadn't been for Abigail and Suzie."

"And look at the trouble that's going to cause. Goodness knows how Dave will say he knew about that. Abigail's not here, is she?" he said worriedly.

"Of course not, hun. They're in the library I expect. I'm meeting them there in the morning so we better get some sleep. I'm totally shattered. I met Suzie's mother today and gave her messages from Suzie. It really took it out of me emotionally."

Tom put his arm around her and kissed her. "One more thing, Tom, I keep getting a vision of a small girl with blonde hair. There isn't one involved in the case, is there?"

"I can check, but I don't think so. Rupert might have kids though. I'll find out for you."

"Oh, one more thing. There's a man called David MacIntosh that has come to our notice in more ways than one. Has anyone mentioned him yet?"

"I've not heard the name. Is he someone important?"

"Apparently. To some of the local ladies. I won't tell you anything, but it will be interesting to see if his name comes up."

"Okay. I'll bear him in mind." Funnily enough, thought Hayley, that was exactly what she was going to do as she drifted off to sleep!

Unfortunately for Hayley, thoughts of David MacIntosh were not there. All she could picture when she closed her eyes was the pretty young girl with the rose in her hair, a white moses basket and for some reason a cuddly toy. Not a Rupert Bear, but an eerie-looking, hand-knitted rabbit, with very long legs.

Chapter 12

ABIGAIL WAS GETTING VERY IMPATIENT SITTING IN the library waiting for all the others to turn up. The only other spirit there was a small ginger cat called Tiggy, the mother of Luna.

Terry was off checking that no Deads had arrived overnight that needed help, as he had helped Abigail. Where Betty was, she had no idea. Betty had such a large family in life that she could be visiting any one of them. Lillian and Suzie had gone to Little Chortle to make sure Jordan didn't have any trouble from bullies at the start of the school year, and were going to miss the meeting. Just when she was thinking of walking off in a huff, she saw Terry and then Hayley walk in. The library was empty so Hayley didn't have to worry about being seen talking to herself, but she waved to Janette, the librarian and picked up a book to read from if she needed to.

"Betty's on her way," said Terry. "So calm down, Abigail."

"What? I'm perfectly calm. I didn't even notice that you're all thirty-four minutes late."

"Sorry, hun. I had a reading to do over the phone and then

sort Luna out. I'm all yours now. And I bought the Chiltern Weekly that has just come out."

"Brilliant. Sorry, morning, Hayley. Oh good, here's Betty. Is there anything in the paper about the murder?"

"I had a quick look because I wanted to see if our advert was in there, and it was. I only sent it yesterday. That's the beauty of the internet; we don't have to wait for anything. I put it in the personals. Look. It's our agency. Don't ask me why I put it in the paper, but I had to. Just a feeling. Someone's going to see it and ring, someone special. You'll see."

Betty said, "How exciting. I wonder who it will be. It must be something really important, Hayley."

"I wouldn't be at all surprised. We'll just have to wait and see, Betty. But back to the regatta; there's nothing on the front page. But on page four, there's a double spread about the regatta and some pictures. No photos of Leo Spencer; dead or alive. It mostly shows the races and I think I can just make out Ben Manson and Ruth sitting in the stands, but I think it was taken on Saturday because here's one of Nina Moore with the junior sailing races. Then there's a small item at the bottom that says, 'The day was marred by the death of Leo Spencer. Detective Chief Inspector Johnson will be giving a press conference when he has finished his enquiries."

"Nothing else that's interesting?" asked Abigail.

Hayley flicked through it. "Not really. Another crash on the Gorebridge Ring Road. Great Billings won the cricket league. More missing pets. Two men charged with conspiracy to burgle after homes targeted in Northridge. A drug dealer has been arrested. That's about it. I could read you your horoscopes if you like?"

"Nah," said Abigail. "We pretty much know our future, thanks. Can you tell us what Tom had to say instead? I could always be there when he's telling you, and then you wouldn't have to repeat it all."

"Oh yes, Tom would love that. You know what he thinks of spirits hanging about."

"Shame. Just a thought," said Abigail.

Hayley gave them a rundown of what she had learned. "He rang a while ago and said that Nina had rung Sergeant Mills and she's been in today to tell them what she knows. She'll feel a lot better now she's got it off her chest. Hopefully she can make a new start for herself after Leo. She was too young to get involved with a married man that kept her hanging about. I told her there's a new man in her future. And he's got the initials S and K."

"Amazing. Why didn't I ask for your help when I was alive?" said Abigail.

"I don't know. I guess before you came along, I was afraid to say too much to anyone in case I looked foolish. Or I was totally wrong. But get this, Tom said she gave her statement to a new sergeant, called Simon Kramer, who has moved here from Southampton."

Betty exclaimed, "SK, Hayley. Brilliant. That's given me an idea. You should start The DDA - The Deadly Dating Agency."

"I think we get ourselves into enough trouble, Betty, without throwing love into it. That's a much more dodgy territory than murder. I do wonder if it was love at first sight. I must try and keep an eye on Nina to see if I'm right, or give her a nudge in the right direction. I'd like to help her more by solving the case, if we can."

Betty said, "What about me and Willy Morgan? Do you see a future for us?"

"Hmm. Sorry, hun, I don't. I think you're a one-man girl."

"You are so right, Hayley. I loved my John for sixty years. I know it's till death do us part, but not in my case. I'll always be his Betty."

"You'll have to let Willy down gently. Why is that funny, Abi? But I think he'll get over it."

"What about me and Terry? Do we pass the test?"

"I don't know if I'm that good. I would say yes, but then you start arguing and then I think no. One thing for sure, your relationship will never be boring. In my experience, those who laugh together, stay together."

"We do do a lot of that," admitted Terry. "So I'll persevere a bit more. She'd be broken-hearted if I dumped her."

"Don't push your luck," laughed Abigail.

"Now this is very important; Tom said they didn't find that letter from the doctor to Ruth. She must have hidden it so the police didn't find out about her relationship with another man. Tom got around it by telling Johnson that one of the other neighbours called him over and said that the doctor was very friendly with Mrs Spencer and had heard that a letter had been sent. Johnson isn't worried enough to find out who told him. He's only interested in results. Oh, and there's no girl of two or three involved in the case like I've been seeing, so it must be something else. I hope one doesn't go missing suddenly. When I get the chance I'll do some meditating and see if anything else comes to mind."

Betty looked worried. "I worry so much about my grandchildren and great-grandchildren these days. If someone hurt a hair on their head, I'd want to kill them."

Hayley said kindly, "I know what you mean, Betty. Don't worry, it's no one in your family. I don't get the feeling that she's suffering or anything. The truth will suddenly come to me soon, no doubt. I think it's someone younger than your great-grandchildren. I can see a Moses basket, covered in white broderie anglaise, with pink bows in each corner. Although the girl I see, who I've decided to call Rose because she's got one in her hair, is far too old for it. It's more for a newborn baby. All will be revealed soon, I daresay. The strangest thing is that I keep seeing a rabbit toy as well. It's a knitted one, standing upright with long legs and arms, with an orange striped waistcoat and trousers on. Very odd. Maybe it belongs to her. Anyway, let's talk about the case for now. Has anyone got any ideas who the murderer could be?"

Terry said, "I think it might be the obvious ones this time - Rupert and Ruth. I know it usually isn't the most obvious, but that could all be part of their plan. Or maybe it's just one of them."

"I agree, Terry," said Betty. "It's even stevens."

"Who the hell is Ethan Stevens?" asked Abigail.

"No," laughed Betty. "It's even stevens. It means middle for diddle. Six of one and twelve of the other."

Abigail shook her head. "Now I'm even more confused. But I don't think it's either of them. The doctor next door sounds a bit dodgy to me; Doctor Sharma. But there are so many people we haven't met yet. Like him, or Leo's business partner."

Hayley added, "That's his brother, Noah. I wonder if he will inherit the business now."

"Not forgetting the vice commodore and that racing organiser. And someone should check out Ruth's stables. Now, as you know, I don't like to be bossy, so what shall we do next?" asked Abigail innocently.

The others all looked at each other in shock. "Well," started Hayley, "Why don't we each …"

"I was thinking," carried on Abigail, "That someone should go to the marina again, like you and me, Terry. And Hayley, how do you feel about going green?"

"I'm not sure. I'm hoping you mean to ride an e-bike. Hopefully not ride a horse."

"Luckily for you I'm thinking of an electric bike. You might like it and never drive your car again."

"You won't say that when you want a lift somewhere. Like how will you and Terry get to Ottersmill?"

Terry had already thought of that. He was so excited to be

having some alone time with Abigail. "The number twelve bus. Twenty past the hour from outside the Town Hall."

He hoped it would be better than the other date at the pub quiz in the Cricketers, which unfortunately had ended in a fatal poisoning. This one would be special. He would make sure of it. There would be no stabbings, poisoning, blackmailing or violent attacks of any kind. Unfortunately for him, but excitedly for Abigail, he was very wrong.

Suzie and Lillian stood outside Chortle Academy as a stream of children entered. Most, apart from the sixth form, were in their school uniforms which were green blazers, tartan skirts for the girls and black trousers for the boys. Lillian said she could tell the new intake as they were the ones whose blazers looked too large and the skirts were nearly down to their ankles. The little ones reminded Suzie that that should have been her. She would have been walking in the gate with her best friend, Camille. It was her birthday party that she had been going to when she had been knocked down on the crossing.

They eventually found Jordan sitting on a wall with two other boys. He looked relaxed and showed no signs of worry. That was until his bully, Russell, came through the gate and entered the school. He walked ahead of his four friends and looked like he was going to say something to her brother, so Suzie didn't take any chances. Lillian tried to stop her, but she went face to face with Russell and stood on tiptoes. She put a cold hand round his neck and breathed a vapour of frosted breath onto his face.

The shocked boy felt a chill that went straight through to his bones, and took two paces backwards. He somehow got out the words, "I'm sorry, Jordan. We're mates now, right?"

Jordan looked puzzled and said, "Yeah, mates," and looked at his friends and shrugged his shoulders.

Suzie smiled. "He was never one to hold grudges. I think he'll be fine now."

Lillian said, "He's a good sort, like his little sister. Do you want to get going now?"

"I might have a look around. Because of that drunk driver I'll never get to go to big school. I'll always be two years away."

"I'm sorry, sweetheart. Let's go and see some of the new kids. I bet they look tiny against all the bigger ones. You might be glad that you didn't start."

"That's a good idea. It must be hard leaving your little school, where you know everyone and be the oldest and then come here and be the youngest."

They eventually found a class of ones that looked a bit bigger than Suzie herself. The teacher was sitting on the edge of his desk and had given them each a book to read. Suzie noticed it was called The House of Deafening Silence by Emma Francis. She hoped she would be able to read it herself at the library when she got back. Mr Trippett, the teacher, pointed to each child, and after they said their names, he asked them to read aloud to the class. Something Suzie hated doing. She always got her words mixed up when she was nervous. Everyone did well until it was the smallest girl, Anya's, turn. Lillian couldn't help but notice that her uniform didn't look new and her hair was not nicely brushed or in a ponytail like most of the others. She had often seen neglected children at the hospital, and Anya's dirty hands and face made her believe this could be one of those cases.

"They t-took one look at the de...lap house,... then c-c..."

"Get a move on, Anya. We do need to finish at least one chapter today, you know?" said the teacher nastily. Some of the others laughed.

Suzie had found another underling to stick up for. "Leave her alone. She's doing her best." Lillian was worried that she was going to push the teacher off the desk, but she went over to

Anya and put her hand on hers and whispered, "You can do this, Anya."

Anya took a deep breath and thought she could do this. In her head she could hear the words and she just started repeating them. It was as if someone was reading them to her. Gran had told her about guardian angels, could this be one? Before she knew it, she had read a whole page. She had tried to read at home and couldn't concentrate, but now, words she had never seen before came into her mind, just when she needed them. It had always been her dread that she would have to read aloud. Even when she played games, the thought that someone would ask her to read the rules had put her off playing. Not that she had many friends. She could never ask them home, so she was worried about getting close to anyone. The day she had been worried about all through the summer holidays had been worse than she had ever imagined. It was English and she had to read aloud. If it wasn't for her angel, she would have just run out of the class. "Thank you," she whispered as she finished the page.

"Well done, Anya," said the teacher, as he pointed to a boy in the back row.

"She heard me, Lillian. Can you believe it? I never knew I could do that."

"I'm as amazed as you. You saved her, that's for sure. I don't think she can read properly. We don't know what is happening at home, so we could look into that."

"Perhaps Mummy can help. I'll watch out for her from now on."

Lillian felt sorry for anyone that tried to bully Anya in the future, knowing what she had done to Jordan's tormentor.

They both waited for the English lesson to finish and then they followed Anya into the dining room for her first school dinner. Lillian and Suzie weren't surprised that she went and sat at a table on her own and no one joined her. The only ones that went near her were two older girls, who looked like they were going to say something nasty, but Suzie nipped that in the bud, as she told Betty later. Somehow her water had been tipped up, all over her blazer and tartan skirt. Suzie couldn't think how! But then something wonderful, but heartbreaking happened for her. The girl who would have been there that day with her, her best friend, had walked past her, carrying her school dinner. It was a beautiful black girl - Camille.

"Lillian, that's her. That's my best friend, Camille. She looks just the same."

"She looks just like you."

"I know. People used to think we were sisters all the time. I wonder if she's thinking of me."

"I'm sure she is, sweetheart. She would love her best friend to be here with her. Both in your new uniforms and giggling, no doubt."

"We were always laughing. She's on her own too. You know what we've got to do? Somehow we've got to get Anya and her together. It will be perfect. They both need a best friend. But how?"

Then Suzie had an idea. As Camille walked past Anya, Suzie picked up a spoon off her tray and dropped it by Anya, who bent down to pick it up for her. Suzie whispered in her ear, "Ask her if she wants to sit with you."

"Sit with me if you like," suggested Anya, surprised at her own courage.

Camille looked down to see a small, skinny girl sitting on her own. She wasn't sure if she wanted to get mixed up with her. She was a bit scruffy, and being seen with her wasn't going to help her to get friends. But she looked around and saw all the other tables were quite full. "Thank you so much. I've been worrying about eating on my own for days. It's scary, isn't it?"

"Yes," said Anya, without looking at her.

"I'm Camille. How has it been so far?"

Anya shrugged her shoulders. "Okay. I'm Anya."

Camille thought this was going to be hard work. "I had maths. Much harder than I thought."

"I had English. My worst nightmare," said Anya.

"I don't mind English. I don't know anyone here. What about you?" asked Camille.

"No. No one. Except you, I suppose," she said, as she smiled for the first time that day.

"Do you live near here?"

"No, not that close." Anya didn't like to say exactly where she lived in case this girl suggested coming round. She'd got used to keeping it a secret. "Do you live in Chortle?"

"I live in Little Chortle, so I can walk. It's not too far."

"I'm on the other side. Perhaps I could walk home with you later, if that's alright with you," said Anya, who again surprised herself. Where were these ideas coming from?

"I'd like that. I hated walking past all the older ones when I came in, did you?"

"I did. It's much better when you're with someone else. I'll meet you at the gate when the bell goes."

"Great. I shouldn't be on my own actually. My best friend should have been here, but she was killed. We always talked about this day and coming to this school. Her name was Suzie. She was such a lovely person. Too good to live, my mum said."

"That's awful. What happened to her?"

"It was all my fault. If it wasn't for me she'd still be alive."

Suzie couldn't believe what Camille was saying. "Why would she think that, Lillian? She hasn't been feeling guilty all this time, has she?" She stopped talking to listen to what they were saying.

"Why is it your fault?"

"She was on the way to my birthday party. I was going to be

ten and she got knocked down on the crossing. I was so angry because she hadn't turned up, and I said some mean things about her. And then later on that day, her mum phoned and told us what had happened. It was the worst day of my life."

"I'm sorry. You never know what's going to happen, do you? I lost my dad when I was eight and that changed my life." Anya was surprised that she had shared that with her. She was always nervous and found it hard to talk to people. But she felt alright with her. All the same, she wouldn't tell her mum about her new friend, Camille. Mum wouldn't like that, just in case she told her things. But she needn't worry, she'd never tell anyone that.

"I'm so glad we met today, Anya. It was like it was meant to be. I wish you could have met her."

Suzie laid her hand on her best friend's shoulder and said, "Don't worry, Camille, she already has."

Lillian started to walk away. "Come on, let's leave them to talk."

"Do you think they will be okay for the rest of the day?"

"I'm sure." Lillian thought that she pitied the one that hurt Camille, for the rest of her life more than likely. "There's nothing to stop you sitting in on a few lessons. You could learn all sorts of things. And just think, if there's a lesson you don't like, you don't have to go. And best of all—no homework."

"Remind me to find out when PE is. Not for myself, but for Anya. I have a feeling she might need a bit of help from me then. Hope it's netball; I could get a few in the net for her."

"I wish we could help her to read."

"Camille was very good at English. I bet she could give her some lessons. I have a feeling that Anya won't tell her, though."

"We can't interfere too much, Suzie."

"I know. We'll wait and see what happens. I don't want Mummy to do anything yet, but she could in the future."

"No, we can't bring in a social worker. We need to find out what's going on first. We could get Jordan to keep an eye on them. I'm betting him and Sonia never thought about Camille starting today. But I have a feeling Anya has more troubles than all of us put together can deal with."

Chapter 13

AS SOON AS THE LIVERIED CHAUFFEUR PULLED UP outside Luxborough Grange, Adreena felt at home. The manor house stood in the centre of two thousand acres, which Adreena's father, the famous Karl Van Derson, had bought off Viscount Stillforth. It was said that he was forced to sell when he went bankrupt due to gambling debts. The word was that the ruthless businessman had somehow engineered that the vast percentage of what he owed was to Van Derson himself. But that was only hearsay.

It felt even more like home when Scrivens, the butler, shuffled out of the door to meet her.

"Miss Adreena, welcome back. I'll see your bags are brought in and taken up to your room. Your cousin and his wife ask that you join them in the drawing room, and I'll arrange for lunch to be served."

"Thank you, Scrivens. It's marvellous to see you're still here. Luxborough wouldn't be the same without you."

"I'll keep going as long as I can, Miss." Mainly because I can't afford it, he thought. No money or a cottage on the estate like he was promised by old Stillforth. He had saved his wages over the years but it wasn't enough to rent somewhere decent to live.

Adreena was met in the hall by two small boys.

"Goodness, you two have grown. Let me see, Andrew and Philip?"

"Albert and Peter. Did you bring us presents?"

"Of course I did." She turned to Scrivens and whispered, "Get a maid or the chauffeur to go into Becklesfield for me and get some toys for them. Cars or something. Come on, let's go and see Mummy and Daddy."

The boys grabbed a hand each and pulled her into the room where their parents were waiting. Adreena was pleased that it all looked the same. They had kept the grand upholstered chairs and the portrait of her parents still hung above the hand-carved, marble fireplace. After hugs and small talk, Viktor and Harriet asked the question they had been wondering about since they heard the news that she was arriving within the next three hours.

Harriet patted the chair next to hers. "It's lovely to see you, Adreena, but we are a bit surprised you wanted to return so soon after what happened. Is there any reason in particular?"

"Don't worry, I'm not here to contest the will. Daddy had a perfect right to leave Luxborough to you. I agreed with him. It should be full of children."

"I wasn't even thinking of that. I meant coming back so soon after your father died."

"His fall was a few months ago now. Although, if only he hadn't gone down the servants' stairs that time of night he would still be alive. It's nothing to do with that, Harriet. I'm not even sure myself why I'm here. It seemed like a good idea last night when I was feeling lonely and needed some company."

Harriet looked concerned. "Is everything alright? You do look a little thinner." She didn't add, and about ten years older.

"Just lately I've been feeling jumpy and hearing things. I'm wondering if I'm going mad actually. It must be the grief coming through. I just felt I needed family around me. And you know my brother, Casper, he's always too busy with the business. And he's not the most compassionate person, let's face it."

"What about your fiancé, Lewis?"

"He's always working as well. He's up north at the moment, Manchester, I think. Maybe we should move in together, although it seems a poor excuse for that. At least I'd get some sleep. It's been weeks since I slept through the night. I have strange dreams where the covers are being pulled off me and I'm freezing cold. Then I wake up and they're on the floor. I can't think if I'm going crazy or if someone is trying to send me mad."

"I'm sure it's just nerves. My doctor gave me something for it when my mother died. He's in Harley Street, I could give you his number."

"It might come to that, thank you, Harriet. But I'll give it a bit longer. I'll have my lunch and then have a nap."

"Of course, and you know you're welcome here anytime." Adreena felt Harriet's mouth had said the words, but her eyes said something different. Viktor nodded, but could she even trust them? Someone had it in for her, that much she knew. But who could she trust?

Chapter 14

LADY CAROLINE HATTON HAD BEEN VERY BUSY WITH all sorts of charity meetings for the last few days. She was beginning to think she was better off when she was working in London. But she had kept the morning free to visit Heather Lockwood, and if she was in, Ruth Spencer.

She had phoned ahead to tell Heather she was coming, so she was let into the exclusive estate promptly at eleven. Heather had said she would be only too happy to sign one of her cookery books to go in an auction. Caroline had explained that it was for a fund-raising event for St Nicholas School for Girls, where Caroline had herself been a pupil and head girl. One of the parents had donated the use of their villa in Bermuda for two weeks, but the signed book from a television chef would be popular as well.

"Do come in, Lady Hatton. Is the kitchen alright or should we sit in the lounge?"

"Please call me Caroline. And the kitchen is fine."

"Good. I've made the coffee and I've just got a tray of cookies out of the oven."

"They smell heavenly. I hope you didn't go to any trouble for me."

"Not at all. My publisher wants a follow-up book so I'm experimenting constantly. This one is called All Things Sweet & Treats. So you must tell me what you think. I'll give you a signed copy when it comes out."

"Well, I'll be keeping that one for me if these biscuits are in it. Truly scrumptious."

"Let me sign that one for you so I don't forget. How about I write 'May your cakes rise and your weight stay the same'. I always like to put something different."

"Brilliant, thank you. I'm sure there'll be a lot of bids for it. You're very well known now. What's it like living here? There are some beautiful houses. I know I have no right to complain, but I'd love a brand new house like this. It would be all clean and nothing would go wrong, like the electrics or the plumbing. The upkeep at Chiltern Hall is unbelievable and it's always cold."

The answer surprised Caroline. "I hate it. I bought it with the royalties for my book and wish I never had. I was so much happier in my small, dilapidated terraced house. I was near friends and the neighbours were always there for each other. Be careful what you wish for, I say."

"It is a bit isolated, I suppose."

"I'm so lonely, Caroline. Between you and me, I've even started to pay someone to spend time with me. He gives me dance lessons and I know full well that if it wasn't for my money, he wouldn't give me the time of day."

"I'm sure that's not true."

"I assure you it is. It's my own fault. I had good friends, but then I got famous on that television show, so I decided I was too good for them all. But I regret it so much now."

"What are the neighbours like here? Can't you get to know them?"

"They are all younger than me, and I don't see that we have much in common. We nod, that's about it. And talk about the weather of course. I've been meaning to go and see Ruth, she lives over at Cedar Cottage. Her husband was murdered last Sunday."

"Ruth Spencer? Yes, I was actually at the regatta that day."

"Me too. I'd left before then, but I wanted to see David in his race, and I was glad I did as he won."

"Do you mean David MacIntosh? I gave him his cup."

"Yes, I do. He's the one that gives me dance lessons."

"Well, lucky you, Heather. I'm sure he is well worth whatever you pay him. I was thinking of calling in on Ruth, if she's home. I don't think she'd mind me calling unannounced, do you?"

"Her car is there, so she's more than likely at home. I must go soon, myself. Could you give her my condolences and tell her that I will drop her over a cake as soon as I can. I wonder if David has been yet."

"Been to give his condolences? Were they friends then?"

"You could say that. Between you and me, Lady Caroline, I wasn't the only one that was paying for his services!"

After hearing that David and Ruth had been involved, Caroline ate another two biscuits and drank her coffee rather quickly. She made a decision to try and get Heather involved with the other ladies of the county. It didn't seem right that she had no friends anymore. And they were always on the lookout for someone to join their coffee mornings and fundraising committees. Heather would be a perfect addition to the Women's Institute, and they would definitely be alright for the cakes on the stalls at all the fetes if she was to join. So she put the signed book in her car and made her way across to the glass house, as she knew it.

Caroline was somewhat worried when she heard barking

from what sounded like a big dog, but she heard Ruth giving Hector a command to sit and it stopped.

"Lady Hatton, I thought I saw you go into Heather's house."

"She was signing a book for a charity auction for me, and I couldn't leave without saying how sorry I am for your loss."

"Remind me to give you one of our electric bikes for the auction. Would you like to come in, or are you busy?"

"For a while, but only if you don't mind. Shall I take my shoes off?"

"This time last week I'd have said yes. But I've given up now. You should have seen the mess the police made the other day."

"I can imagine, Ruth. What a lovely home."

"Is it? I think I hate it here."

"Do you know, that's exactly what Heather said? She sends her regards and will be coming over with a cake when she can."

"That's kind of her. Would you like coffee?"

"No, thank you. I've just had one and a plateful of biscuits."

"I'll get you some wine then."

"Only if you join me."

"No, I won't today. Please take a seat, Lady Caroline." They sat on a white leather sofa.

"Have the police caught whoever did it yet?"

"I think they suspect me, and they have been questioning poor old Rupert, which is totally ridiculous. He would never be able to hurt anyone. And if he ever did, I'm sure he would be able to come up with a less traceable murder, seeing as he is a Queen's Counsel barrister."

"I don't think I know him."

"He's a close friend of mine and has a boat at the marina."

"As you know, I was at the regatta that day. Not that I could tell the police anything. I was in the stands and then giving out the prizes." She was trying to get the subject round to David MacIntosh. If he was seeing Leo's wife, that would be a good reason for a fight between the two, which might have got out of hand. And she was a very beautiful woman. "I gave one to a really good looking rower. His name was David, I think. He won the Hatton Cup. Do you know the one I mean?"

"I know David. He's very friendly with your friend, Heather as well. And I saw him myself at one time. It's not like you think though. It wasn't an affair and it was over a year ago. I needed something else from him at the time. And when he knew what I really wanted, he turned me down. So he didn't do everything for money."

"Sailing lessons?"

"Not even close, Lady Caroline. I wasn't the only one. A lot of the pony club mums use his services."

"No! I don't believe it. Not Bridget Thomson-Jones, surely?"

"My lips are sealed, but yes, you're right."

Caroline shook her head. "Well, I'm shocked. She's the most pious of them all. I think you should know that Heather was actually using David for ballroom dancing. I can't tell you how I know, so don't say anything."

"What a good idea. I must invite her for a coffee one of these days, if I'm not locked up. What about you? How well did you know David, if you don't mind me asking?"

"I've never felt the need to pay yet, and I don't think I have the time," laughed Caroline. "I'd better make a move. Please get in touch if there's anything I can do to help, Ruth."

"I will, but I'm fine, thank you."

Caroline thought that she was fine, and that was the strange thing. Her husband had just been murdered and she was fine. What was going on? She was so pleased that she had plenty to tell Hayley and the others.

Chapter 15

Hayley sat at the kitchen table having her lunch and wondering if she should go to the bike factory first, or the stables. She wasn't really in the mood for either. It was alright for Abigail and the others, they didn't have to worry about mundane things like shopping or housework. And she had got behind with her therapy jobs. There were three people she had to get back to that wanted tarot readings and guidance.

In the end she decided to visit Estryke Bikes first, even though it was further away. Mainly just in case she trod in something at Ruth's stables. For the first time in a while she put on trousers. She had looked up the firm online and there was somewhere you could try out one of the bikes. So trousers and trainers it would have to be, rather than her long skirt and sandals. Maybe she should put her boots in the car for the stables. And whatever Abigail said, there was no way on earth that she would get on a horse.

Luna could tell with all the activity that he was going to be left on his own again. One of his servers had already left for wherever he went every day, and now the other one was rushing around. The woman had been having a shower and putting things on her face before she had even fed him, or given him his morning fuss, if you please! You can't get the staff these days. And the speed she was now putting a pouch of food in his bowl, he knew he'd not be getting any tickles, let alone a game or two.

All Luna actually got was a quick scratch behind the ears and something about going to see a man about a horse. She could forget that! Luna sat on the windowsill and watched as his owner drove away. Oh well, he'd have a quick nap and then do some chores. The furniture doesn't get scratched, or those ornaments pushed off the side on their own!

Hayley drove through heavier than usual traffic on the Gorebridge Ring Road. She thought she would have to go around again at this rate, but then she saw a vast building with the large letters 'Estryke' in green. She pulled up outside the showroom, where there were models of all the different bikes on show in the window.

A middle-aged woman was sitting at a desk to welcome any potential buyer.

"Morning. Have you got an appointment?"

"No, I'm actually just popping in on the off chance I could have a look at your bikes. I've decided to go green."

"Good for you. Do you know which one you want?"

"An electric one, or the colour do you mean?"

"No. They're all electric. There's more choice than the colour." She got out from behind the desk. "There's the size of the wheels. These ones are foldable. They're very good if you have to commute on a train. Or for holiday if you have a caravan or a boat. Or there are these with a rack on the back for carrying goods or even for taking the children on the school run."

"Goodness. I thought a bike was a bike. Probably a very small folding one then. I like the fact that the wheels are smaller. I haven't ridden one for years. This one looks good."

"Okay. I'll get one of the salesmen. You can try one out if you like. I think you'll be impressed, Ms?"

"Hayley's fine. Is Noah in today?"

"He is. Do you know him?"

"Only through a friend of a friend," Hayley lied. "I'm surprised he's here after his sad loss."

"We all are, but he's going to be even busier now he's running the company on his own. Leo wouldn't have wanted the sales to suffer. Noah said he preferred to be here than on his own. I'll see if he's free." She picked up the phone and within two minutes Noah Spencer had come through from the back.

He was good looking as well, but Hayley wasn't sure how much he looked like his older brother, as she had never met him. An orange folding bike was selected and Noah and Hayley went outside to a track that ran down the side of the factory.

He handed her a black helmet, which worried Hayley slightly. How dangerous was this thing? And how fast would it go? And more importantly, would she know how to stop it?

Noah switched it on from the controls on the handlebars and Hayley started pedalling to the sound of a slight whirring noise. She did a loop and rode back to a smiling Noah.

"That was amazing. I love it. I felt totally in control and the pedals went round so easily. You know when you first get on and start pedalling when it wobbles, there was none of that. Amazing."

"Everyone says that. They are good, aren't they?"

"Brilliant. I'm going to get my husband to try one. We could have a whole new hobby for the weekends. I would never have believed how easy they are to handle. And I felt safe. They're a bit more money than I would have liked though."

"You can spread the cost if you like. We do very good terms."

"I'm very impressed. And I hope I won't upset you, but I want to tell you how sorry I am about your brother, Leo. A friend of mine, Lady Caroline Hatton is friends with Ruth. It must be the worst time for you all."

"Thank you, it is. It doesn't help that it's such a busy time at the moment. Sales are always highest in the summer."

"I can imagine. The nice weather makes you want to get out there. I suppose the company belongs to Ruth now, does it?" Hayley said, hoping to touch a nerve.

"No, actually it's mine after Leo's death. Whoever went first, the other would inherit. Ruth will carry on getting a small percentage but that's all."

"Oh, I'm sorry. I didn't know you were the co-owner. Caroline didn't mention that. But I suppose Ruth has got the stables to keep her busy."

"Yes, thankfully. To be honest, I haven't seen her since it happened. We were never that close."

Hayley was worried about asking too many questions, but she decided to carry on. "Were you at the regatta when it happened? That must have been dreadful for you. I'm so sorry."

"I was in the morning. I went with my girlfriend and she had to get back. I didn't speak to Leo though; he was too busy. You don't know how much I wish I had. I can't stand to think I'll never have the chance again. And Leo might still be alive today."

"We can never know. Do you have any idea who might have killed him?" This proved to be one question too many for the grieving brother.

"No, I don't! Why are you so interested anyway? I've had enough of this from the police and the journalists, without you giving me the third degree. Do you want this bike or not?"

"I need to speak to my husband first, but I think they're great. I apologise for upsetting you just now, Noah. The trouble is, I always think that I can help people. I do it for a living."

"Are you a kind of counsellor?"

"No. I'm a kind of medium."

Hayley made her excuses and left soon after she had surprised Noah with her occupation. It made him clam up even more, so she promised to talk about buying a bike with her husband and then she joined the busy Gorebridge Ring Road once more. Noah knew she wouldn't be back.

She had no idea where Cranston Stables were, so she put the postcode into the satnav. She knew it was the other side of Becklesfield, but it would be so easy to get lost in the lanes that criss-crossed that area. It told her she had another twenty minutes of driving until she arrived at her destination. Hayley was very pleased that she had used technology to find the stables. It would have been impossible without. The stables were a mile from the village of Cranston and down a dirt track off a hidden lane, with no signposts.

The first thing she saw was a large farmhouse with green-painted window frames and doors. Hayley immediately felt drawn to it. One of the rooms upstairs on the right seemed to be calling to her more than the others. The house looked at least a hundred years old, but the stables looked relatively new. Either that, or they had been recently renovated. Hayley parked by some four-wheel-drive vehicles and opened the red, five-bar gate that led to the courtyard. On each side of her were stalls with the names of horses written above. Cobweb and Poppet were looking back at her, wondering if this was someone that was going to let them have their freedom for an hour or two. Hayley was glad that she didn't stop to put her boots on as the area looked immaculate.

A young stable-girl came out to greet her. "Did you want something? This is a private area. It's bookings only, I'm afraid."

Hayley had no idea how to play this one. Usually, she had it all planned. It wasn't like she could say she wanted to buy a horse like she did the bike. And if she said she wanted to ride one, she might actually have to do it.

"Er, actually, I was hoping I could see Ruth." She just hoped that she wasn't there.

"She's not in today. There's been a death in the family."

"I know. That's why I'm here."

An older lady came out of one of the stables carrying a saddle and bridle. "Can I help you? I'm Ruth's mother. I don't remember having seen you with her. But come up to the house, I'll get you a drink. Can you hang these up, please, Milly." Hayley followed her along the path and through a smaller gate, which took them round to the back door. Hayley felt the pull stronger as she got closer.

"I love your house. I feel it has a lifetime of history."

"It was built in about the eighteen-fifties originally. But it's had bits built on over the years. There were only two rooms to start with and no upstairs. I'm Diane Parry."

"I'm Hayley."

"I know who you are," which took Hayley aback. "I saw you do that demonstration for the Women's Institute. It was very good. You're Hayley Moon, the psychic. I know all about what you do."

"Then you know I mean no harm to either of you. I want to help if I can. And now I'm here, I'm feeling some very strange vibes from the house itself. I'm not sure why."

"I think I know why. And I'm pleased you came. I can't think how you've got involved, but I'm glad you are. How much do you know about Ruth and her history, and her illness?"

"I know nothing at all, Diane. I've had some visions lately that I haven't been able to understand, but that's about it. Forgive me if I'm wrong, but one of the visions I see is of a little girl. I'm starting to understand. It's Ruth's little girl I'm seeing, isn't it?"

"So you do know. It must be little Patricia Rose. Ruth lost her husband and her daughter together, in a car accident eight years ago. The little angel was only three. Ruth was never the same. She came to live here with me in the end."

Hayley hoped that DCI Johnson wouldn't find out about her first husband. No doubt he would think to lose one is an accident, to lose two is murder. She needed to help her even more somehow.

"There's a room upstairs, can I see it, Diane? It feels important." Diane led the way up a narrow staircase and opened the door. It was a shrine to Patricia Rose. A large rocking horse filled one wall and in the corner was what Hayley had been expecting - a moses basket covered in white broderie anglaise and with a pink bow in each corner. Above a mound of cuddly toys, on a shelf, was a large photograph of Patricia Rose, with a flower in her hair.

Hayley went over and picked up the pink frame. "I've seen this photograph and this room, Diane. Poor Ruth. I'm not sure if it means that I have to do something for her, but I've seen it for a reason."

"After Patricia and Ian died she stayed in their big house, but she couldn't cope. She kept cleaning and cleaning, herself and the house. We learned after that it was OCD and germophobia brought on by the grief and shock. We had no idea at the time what was happening. But when she didn't have the strength to clean anymore, she went into full depression and the house began to decay with her mind. She wouldn't let anyone in, physically or mentally. She sold up and moved in here with me after I begged her time and time again. This room has stayed the same since Patricia used to come here and it gave her some comfort."

"Did she get some proper help?"

"Yes. I don't think she'd be here now if she hadn't, Hayley. Doctor Sharma was her saviour. They became the best of friends, actually."

"Is that Doctor Sharma that lives next door to her now?"

"Yes, that's the one. You do seem to know a lot."

"It must have made a difference when she met Leo. Had she recovered by then, Diane?"

"She met him at one of her hospital visits and they got talking. I was so surprised she was interested in anyone, but they hit it off. She started getting out of the house anyway, so I was pleased. She started to recover slowly after that. But I don't think she was ever as happy as when she was with Ian. I think it was more a marriage of convenience. She was, and still is, desperate for another child, and he wanted the money to start his bike business. He got plenty off his friends and family, but mainly off Ruth. So Leo got his wish but Ruth didn't get her little girl. Or even a boy."

"Is that why she was having an affair, do you think? If Leo couldn't give her what she wanted so badly, she tried elsewhere?"

"I'm sure of it. Ruth would have done anything to get pregnant. She wouldn't have wanted to have an affair otherwise. I'm just worried that the police will find out about her mental troubles and make out she's a homicidal maniac."

"They wouldn't do that," but Hayley knew that DCI Johnson would be more than capable of making that leap. "How is she coping with Leo's death? Do you think it will set her back to where she was?"

"It's always at the back of my mind. But so far she seems fine. Contented even. There's none of that deep depression like before."

"It must be a comfort to know that Doctor Sharma is only next door to her. That will help. At one time, I'm guessing they were closer than doctor and patient. Am I right?"

"They were very close. She meant the world to Ruth and she relied on her far too much at one point."

"She? Her doctor was a she?"

"Yes. I thought you knew. Her husband is a GP and she is a renowned psychiatrist."

Well that's one mystery solved, thought Hayley. She realised that Ruth must have hidden the letter, not to hide an affair, but so Johnson didn't find out about her seeing a psychiatrist. Hayley walked over to the toys and touched a soft white bear with a pink bow around its neck.

"Me and my husband bought that when Patricia was born and took it to the hospital."

"I can feel the love. This will sound strange, but did you knit her a white rabbit?"

"Me, knit? Not with these hands. I tried to learn when I was about ten, but my mother gave up. Why?"

"I just wondered. Nothing important. I wish I could tell you that I feel your granddaughter is close, but I don't, Diane."

"I know. We went to a Spiritualist Church when it happened and we were told then that she had passed over with her daddy and was safe and happy. But that just made Ruth more depressed and even angry that Ian had her and she didn't. She wanted to be the one that had died. The mind is a strange thing. I think she should move back here for a while, don't you? In case she relapses."

"I get the feeling that that would be for the best. She'll feel safe here, and it's a lot more homely than the house in Edenbury Heights."

Diane smiled briefly. "They call it Millionaire's Row, but to me it looks and feels like an open prison. Hector will be happier here as well. He's actually my dog, but she took it with her because she didn't feel safe there when Leo went away, even with all the security. So much glass, how could it possibly feel safe?"

"I totally agree. Give me my little cottage anytime. And this house is full of love and warmth. She really needs to come home. I sense that many families have grown up in bliss."

"They have. It's been in my late husband's family for many generations."

"Keep it to yourself, Diane, but I have some friends that are trying to find out who killed your son-in-law, so don't worry. We're going to make sure that the right person is put away, and as quickly as possible," Hayley said as they left the bedroom.

Once she'd got back in the car, she leaned back and rested her eyes. Learning about what Ruth had been through had drained her, and she needed to think of something positive. She'd go and find Abigail. She was the most positive person that she knew. Hayley put the car into reverse and set off for Ottersmill Marina to see what she and Terry had been up to.

Chapter 16

"So, Terry, are you going to take me on a boat or what?" asked Abigail, as they watched a small sailing boat pass them.

"I know you'll laugh, but I can't swim."

"But you can't drown," laughed Abigail.

"I know that, but I could sink and never be seen again," he said seriously.

"Really? I hadn't thought of that. We'd better not risk it then."

"Let's sit here for a while and watch the boats go by. It's kinda romantic."

Abigail agreed. "I know. What is it about water? The beach is the same. I remember walking on the sand with Bruce Biggley in our bare feet. I thought he was going to propose at last. But the only thing he proposed was to get fish and chips and eat them on the sea wall. Not even in a restaurant. The story of my life."

"I wish I'd known someone like you when I was alive. Did I tell you that I think you're beautiful and clever? Admittedly you'd have driven me up the wall, but I would have put up with that."

"Oh, Terry, you know all the right things to say to a girl. I can't for the life of me think why you never married!"

"I never asked anyone. I woulda you though. Mainly to stop you chasing me. You wouldn't have been able to resist my charms, Abigail Summers."

"Is that right? I might have turned you down, Terry Styles."

"Nah. You'd be putty in my hands. And after you'd said 'Yes, I'd love to marry you, Terry. I'm so lucky,' I'd take you in my arms and would have said..."

"JUMP. Quick, you idiot. You're supposed to take the bloody rope with you." A young couple that didn't seem to know what they were doing, had pulled alongside them on a rented day-boat.

"I swear to God, Abigail, one day we'll have the perfect date with no interruptions."

"The day's not over yet. Let's go and find that Willy Morgan and then we're done. Then we can relax. You met him, what does he look like?"

"An old boy. Betty says he's got a flat cap like in that show that's on. Some comedy or other. I think she said it's set in Birmingham in the old days and she'd get Suzie to put it on one night. It had a funny name. Er, The Cheeky Peakies or The Sneaky Peakies."

"The Sneaky Peakies? That ain't no comedy show. Betty should never ever watch that. It's actually called... Oh look, there he is. She's right though, he does look like one of them."

"Morning. Nice day," said Willy.

Terry shook his hand. "Sorry to bother you again. This is Abigail Summers."

"Hello, Willy. The famous detective, if you've ever heard of me."

"No, can't say I have. But I don't get out much."

"Shame, but never mind. We need to ask you about the man

who died here on Sunday. I heard that you saw him just after he'd died."

"I did that. He was soaking wet with a cut on his head, so I just thought, there's another one that fell in."

"Did you recognise him, Willy?"

"I'd seen him about, but they all look the same, these rich ones. I don't go near the bar. It's like living in purgatory, seeing all that drink and not being able to have a drop. I keep to the river. Boats are my thing; not people."

"Now, this is important. When he said, 'It's mine,' was he saying it like, get off, it's mine, or grabbing it like, it's mine. And was he angry or surprised or happy even? Or was it like a 'my precious ring' thing?"

"I don't know what you mean about a 'precious ring' thing." Willy thought for a moment. "I would say he was happy. Or as happy as a dead man could be. Which made it a very strange thing for a murdered man to say."

"Yes, it is. That is very helpful. Terry, it might be starting to make sense." Not to him, thought Terry.

"Is that it then?" asked Willy. "Where's the good-looking one? I think it was Betty. I was hoping she'd be with you."

Terry said, "She's back at the library and then she had to visit her daughter. I'm sorry. Hopefully, she can come next time, Willy."

"Good. I liked her. My kind of woman. Good sense of humour too."

Abigail felt a bit jealous after being passed over for an octogenarian, if that was the right word. Now even Betty would be chatted up and have more dates than her.

"We'll give her your message and see if we can get her to visit. Thank you so much for your help, Willy. We'll all visit again when we can," Terry promised.

The old man walked slowly away, up towards the willow tree where he knew the ducks and swans were waiting. Willy

Morgan preferred their company to humans, alive or dead. Apart from that Betty; he would make an exception for her.

"Betty has still got it then apparently," said Terry.

"Well, I suppose we could double-date," laughed Abigail. "There's hope for me then, if she can still pull at eighty-two."

"Yeah, you've got a few more years left."

"Ha ha, very funny. I have a feeling that I saw something important last time I was here. But it will come to me, I hope. Come on then, let's go and mingle," Abigail said as she grabbed Terry's hand and led him back towards the clubhouse. It was then that they heard the screaming and shouting.

Here we go again, thought Terry. Seriously, every time he tried to get romantic something happened. What was it this time, he wondered. Someone hacked to death with a pickaxe?

Abigail was in her element, however, and raced through the people and tables like a thing possessed, as Terry told the others afterwards. It was a strange scene that awaited them. No corpse, which was a plus, thought Terry.

A group had gathered in the fenced-in yard at the back of the club. Sitting on the ground by the bins was Moira. She had a rope around her neck and was crying and shouting, "He tried to kill me!" Who, she didn't say. David MacIntosh was standing by her and said the gate was open when he heard the screams and got to her.

"Whoever it was had gone. She was lying on the floor and I thought she was dead."

Her husband, Barry, helped her to her feet and carried her back into the kitchen. He told David to call the police and get an ambulance. He sat his wife down and asked her, "Who did this to you, Moira?"

She started to cough and her voice went croaky. "I didn't see who it was. I heard the gate open and before I could turn I felt the rope go round my neck, and just managed to get my fingers behind the rope. I blacked out and that saved my life. He must have thought that I was dead."

Abigail passed through Barry, who felt a sudden chill as if someone had walked over his grave. She took a close look at Moira's wounds and wished Lillian was there to give her professional opinion. Abigail could see a red mark around the throat and vertical scratches on the front of the neck where Moira had clawed at the rope. "Hayley warned you," she said to the oblivious Moira.

Rupert and some of the others appeared in the kitchen from the bar and said, "How is she?" to Barry. Abigail thought it strange that Rupert didn't ask what had happened.

"Okay, I think. We need to leave this place. I've had enough now. They don't pay enough for this."

Vice Commodore Gail Fletcher said, "Oh please don't, Barry. We've already lost Leo and Ruth this week. The club will have to shut if you do."

"I don't care. Look what someone's done to my wife, Gail."

Tom and WPC Jane Nichols were the next to arrive and asked Barry, "What's happened? We'd just arrived when we got the call."

"Someone tried to kill my wife. Moira was putting the rubbish out when someone came in the gate and tried to kill her. If you'd have done your job and caught him, this would never have happened."

Abigail would have loved to tell Tom that it could have been someone from the club who did it and then went out the gate. She needn't have worried.

Tom said, "Or he or she could have gone out through that door and then run out the gate. I'm sorry, the whole place is the crime scene. Mrs Potts, you'll have to be checked out at the hospital. The ambulance is on its way. Jane, get everyone in the bar and don't let anyone leave the marina at all. I'll get the tape out of the car. Dave Mills is sending some more uniforms to help. DCI Johnson is coming as well."

"God, not him. That's all we need. Can I go to the hospital with my wife, please, Constable? She's obviously traumatised."

"I'm sorry, sir, no. We'll need your statement most of all."

"You can't think that I'm guilty, for God's sake."

"Until we know where everyone was, everyone is a suspect, sir." Abigail felt very proud of young Tom. He would make an excellent detective, if only Johnson would retire or get sacked.

Tom excused himself as he'd just noticed someone out of the corner of his eye.

"Hayley, what the hell are you doing here?" He felt a waft of freezing cold air and knew that she wasn't alone. "You can't be here, Johnson's on his way. Go quick and don't let anyone see you go. Whip out the back through the kitchen, but don't touch anything out there. It's the primary crime scene. They've all been told to stay, so you'll get everybody complaining if I've allowed you to go. So hurry up."

"I just got here. Nina's over there. Can I just have a quick word?"

"No, you can't. Go. I'll see you at home later."

Abigail, Terry and Hayley had a quick look at the crime scene and then headed for the Mini. When the sirens could be heard, they were well on their way back to Becklesfield.

Chapter 17

Back at Hayley's house, Lillian, Suzie and Betty had joined the others and were shocked to hear what had happened to Moira.

Lillian pointed her finger at Hayley. "See. It just shows how careful you have to be. That could be you next. She must have been getting close to knowing who it was."

"Not necessarily, hun. She was stupid enough to say in front of everyone in the bar that she was going to find out who killed Leo. Nina and Barry were there, and I'll have to try and remember who else. At least we've narrowed it down to someone from the club. But I suppose anyone could have parked at the back and gone in the gate. Whoever it was will be shocked to see that she's still alive. Good job that gorgeous David was passing by."

Betty said, "Ah, but was he passing by or there to kill her and ran back in to say that he saved her? So he must have been shocked if it was him. What do you think, Abigail?"

"He wasn't the only one there. Rupert Cox got there very quickly from somewhere."

"I've got so much to tell you about Ruth that I learned today.

And Lady Caroline popped over there as well and gave me a very interesting update. I'll give you more details later, but the sad thing is that Ruth's mother told me that Ruth lost her husband and little girl in a car accident. That was the picture that I was seeing. It was her daughter, Patricia. She was only having an affair with Rupert as she was desperate for another baby and she hadn't fallen pregnant with Leo. But the knitted rabbit I keep seeing has got nothing to do with her, so am I seeing it because of this case?"

"Hmm. Do we know anyone with long legs and an orange waistcoat?" asked Betty.

"No one I can think of. But there were a few others there. Obviously Barry, the Vice Commodore and Ben Manson. Not forgetting your gigolo. His legs were quite long, and the waistcoat could be a lifejacket," said Terry.

"That is a bit of a stretch, to be honest. But I saw Nina Moore too, hun. We can't know who has an alibi though, so we'll have to wait until we hear from Tom."

"I hate all this waiting about," said Abigail. "I've worked something out but we can't do much till I find something out. I don't suppose you would run me and Suzie over to Ruth's house, would you, Hayl?"

"I can drop you at the gate, but that's it. Be careful though, I think she's home today. She's not at the stables, I do know that."

"I haven't got to go inside," Abigail told her confused friends.

"I bet you know who did it," said Suzie. "You're as good as that Sherlock Holmes I've been reading about."

"I only know one part of it. I have no idea who the murderer is yet. If anything, I've just complicated things in my mind."

Hayley held up a hand to quiet them as she looked at her phone. "You won't believe this. I've just had the first email for our detective services on the website. Hang on, let me read it."

The Deadly Regatta

"I bet it's a lost cat," said Abigail.

Suzie said, "It's sad for someone, but sooo boring."

Hayley put down her phone. "Well, that's where you're wrong for a change, Abigail Summers. It's a lost dog!"

After telling them all she had learned about Noah Spencer and Ruth, Hayley dropped Abigail and Suzie at Edenbury Heights and waited up the road for them. She had no idea what they were looking for. Whatever it was, Abigail said she would share in her own time. Then a van pulled up to the large, imposing gates and an arm reached out and pressed a few buttons. The double gates swung open and then it pulled over outside the big glass house.

"Now that is interesting. I'm sure he told Tom he didn't know Leo. So why did he lie?"

Hayley got out her phone and took a picture of him getting out of his van. Written on the side was 'Redman's Windows & Gutters'.

Inside Cedar Cottage, Ruth Spencer looked out of her many windows to see that the window cleaner had arrived. But then she saw a surprising sight. The wind must have suddenly got up. Why else would her bin lid have raised on its own and bits of rubbish flew out? Then somehow it was blown in again. Must be global warming or a mini tornado, she thought.

Hayley couldn't wait to tell Tom that night about seeing Mr Redman at Ruth's house. It seemed a bit suspicious that he had been the one to pull the body out of the river and he said he didn't know him. She couldn't tell him what Suzie had found because she didn't know. Even Suzie didn't know what it was, as Abigail wanted to keep it to herself. Whatever it was, she had left it there for the police to find if it was needed for evidence. But she looked very pleased with herself. Or as Betty had remarked, 'Like the cat that's got the pigeon out of the bag.'

Tom had quite a lot of news of his own to pass on, however. Because DCI Johnson had arrested Rupert Cox. He was the only one, apart from Nina Moore, who didn't have an alibi at the time of Moira's attack. He didn't consider Nina as she was much shorter than Moira, and it was unlikely that she had the strength. Rupert had told them that he was on his boat, down below, but Jack said he had seen him out of the chandlery window. The rope that was around Moira's neck even matched the one that was coiled up on his pontoon.

Moira had been checked over and been allowed to go home after a few hours. She had been advised to go to a hotel, but didn't want to. She couldn't add anything else to her statement. She was at the bins when someone opened the gate and wrapped the rope around her neck from behind. She couldn't say if he went out the gate or in through the door of the club that she had left open, as she had blacked out by then.

Hayley had to wait until the morning to pass on the news to the rest. They were meeting at hers and she knew exactly what Abigail would say to the arrest of Rupert Cox. The clean version would be 'bull manure'.

And as good as Abigail was, she had forgotten that Hayley was even better at what she did. She could investigate in her own spiritual way. Oh no, Abigail wasn't the only one who had worked out the good news, that Ruth was having a baby.

Chapter 18

ADREENA WAS WIDE AWAKE AGAIN. SHE HAD BEEN since three o'clock. It was her second night at Luxborough and things hadn't improved. The first night she had the idea of taking Maxwell, the black Labrador, to bed with her. That was even worse because whenever she did drop off, he would keep barking and there wasn't anything there. She had gone to sleep quite quickly for her, even with the bright lamp on, but soon after she shivered with the chill in the air, and then felt the bed go down next to her. Adreena was convinced someone had sat down, but there was no one there. She heard the thud of footsteps that led to the door and inexplicably carried on down the landing. Whoever was doing this was good, she thought. But she'd never believed in ghosts and wasn't going to start now. She put her head under the covers, but sleep never came.

Adreena had never felt so pleased to hear the dawn chorus and see the sun coming up. She looked at the clock on the nightstand, just as movement seemed to come from the huge wardrobe in the corner of the room. So the terrified woman thought it would be a good time to get up. She knew the servants rose early, but they knew not to take her an early morning tray of tea, as normally she liked to lie-in till mid-morning. So she put on her dressing gown and left her room. Scrivens wouldn't be about, but that new maid would probably be going around pulling the curtains. She tiptoed along to the grand staircase, not wanting to talk to Harriet if she was awake. Nor did she want to wake up the boys. It was definitely too early for children, especially those two. On the second step, something caught her eye as she put her foot down. She lost her footing and just managed to grab the bannister. She gasped and held on tight with both hands. Both of which were shaking. That was far too close. That hadn't been done by any ghost or practical joker. Someone had woken her and deliberately placed those on there for one purpose only - her death. Adreena picked up the boys' wooden cars and put them in her pocket. The fact that she had bought them herself made her even angrier. This was no accident. This was attempted murder. They didn't want her locked up; they wanted her dead.

She walked slowly down the stairs, checking every step and made it to the bottom. She was frightened someone was going to push her. She stopped to listen, but the only sound was the ticking of the grandfather clock. A light flashed by the hall table and she noticed the Chiltern Weekly was on it. Adreena wasn't the type to read a newspaper, especially not a local one, but something in her head made her pick it up, or had a breeze lifted one of the pages? Looking around to make sure that no one was following her, she took it into the library and pulled the cord that rang the bell in the servant's hall, for the maid to bring her a tray of tea. Adreena settled down in a chair that was facing the door and opened the newspaper. Amazingly, the first thing she saw was an advert for The Deadly Detective Agency.

Chapter 19

ABIGAIL WAS REALLY LOOKING FORWARD TO THE meeting at Hayley's house. She had found what she thought she might find last night at Ruth's house, and a few other things were starting to take shape. She still wasn't sure exactly who had done what yet, but she knew she soon would. Terry and Suzie were walking with her to Hayley's house in Church Lane and were just passing the village green when Abigail grabbed Terry's arm.

"Look. There's David MacIntosh. What's he doing here?"

"Talking to Reverend Pete and Mary by the looks of it. I wonder why. Whatever he said to them, they walked off pretty sharpish."

"Come on, let's follow him."

"Hmm. I thought you might say that." But David went and sat on the wall by the churchyard.

Abigail stopped in front of him. "He really is hot."

"Oh please," said Terry. "You're old enough to be his…"

"Watch it!"

"Sister?" said Suzie.

"Exactly. But seriously, Terry, look at those…"

"Excuse me, are you talking to me?" They all looked around to see who David was looking at. But then they realised that he was talking to them.

"You can see us?" asked Abigail.

David held out his hands. "Now we've all established that we can see each other, could you tell me what the hell has happened to me, please?"

Terry put on his voice reserved for talking to the newly Deads. "Well, son, this is going to be hard for you, being as you're so young. And don't worry it's not…"

"You're dead," said Abigail. "What? He had to know."

David put his head in his hands. "I had a feeling I was. I remember walking along and the next thing I know I'm here. Where is this? Heaven?"

"Not quite. Becklesfield," said Abigail bluntly.

"But it's very nice," said Suzie. "You can stay at the library with us."

Terry wasn't so sure about that, so he was quite pleased when David said, "I'm not really a library person, shorty. I don't think I've even been in one since I left school. Why am I dead, do you think?"

"Turn around, let's look at you. Ah. Was your head always flat at the back?" asked Abigail.

"Not that I know of." He felt it with his left hand. "Not that flat anyway, I'm sure. Do I know you, or do you know me?"

"You're David MacIntosh, the g… great rower. Come with us back to our friend's house. She's a medium and don't worry, between us we're going to work out exactly who did this. You've come to the right place. I need to pick your brain about what happened at the marina." To anyone else Abigail would have said, 'what's left of it,' but it did seem a bit too soon, and she had the feeling that David MacIntosh did not have much of a sense of humour.

Nobody was more surprised than Hayley to see David

MacIntosh in her sitting room. After all the introductions had been made, they began to discuss this new murder.

"I think the fact that my husband, Tom, who's a policeman, hasn't told me, means that your body hasn't been found yet, David."

"You're not wet, so you're not floating in the river like Leo was. And you might have been killed anywhere," said Terry.

"I'm going to get Tom to drop some hints to the sergeant and get him to do a search. He knows I've helped in cases before, you see. Do you know when it happened? What's the last thing you remember, hun?"

"Pretty much all day yesterday I was kept at the marina after the attack on Moira. We all had to say where we were and who we were with. It was a bit awkward for me because I was on my own without an alibi, and actually on the spot soon after. I'd parked up the back lane and was walking towards the boathouse to have a row when I heard the screams. So I had to admit to the police that I saw no one and no one saw me. And I was shut in this room with a horrible little policeman, Johnson, I think. And he was being deliberately obtuse."

Betty waded in. "But, David, it's not their fault when they're overweight. My John had an eating problem through no fault of his own when he was younger. But as he got older he lost it."

David's eyes widened and he said, "What the…"

"Finish what you were telling us, David, please." Abigail wasn't going to let this stranger have a go at their Betty, bless her little cotton socks. Oh no, she's got me at it again, she thought. That was one of her old nan's sayings.

David gave a shake of the head and carried on. "But I was off the hook, as they say, when they arrested Rupert Cox, if you know who that is? That awful detective hauled him off, so the rest of us were so relieved we all went in the club, and had too much to drink. Gail and I served the drinks while Barry went and picked up Moira, so it was doubles all round. Then Barry put Moira to bed and let us stay after hours."

"If you were sozzled, do you think you could have fallen and hit your head?" asked Terry.

"Maybe. But when I've done that in the past, I've gone face first. I would have rung up for a taxi if I'd been that drunk, so I have no idea where I was when I left the bar."

Abigail frowned. "Do you think someone said you could stay on their boat? Nina Moore has a boat there, do you think she invited you?"

"Could have. I know she hasn't got Leo anymore, and she had been knocking back the vodkas as well."

Hayley's phone went and they all stopped talking to listen. "Hi, Tom. You did? I was just about to ring you actually. You're not going to believe it, but he's here. David is. Yes, in the conservatory. Oh, you do believe it. No, he hasn't got a clue who hit him. It's all a bit hazy. I'll let you know if we learn anything. We'll talk soon. Bye, hun. They've found you. A walker saw something and phoned it in. You were in the lane, on the verge, hidden in some bushes. A branch with your blood on it was thrown nearby. It was definitely murder. And you still have no idea who hit you?"

"None at all. I wish I did. I'd go straight there and give them hell, believe me."

Hayley asked, "Have you any idea who killed Leo? Perhaps you were killed for something to do with that."

"I assume it was Rupert now."

"The only fly in the ointment with that is that he was in custody when you were attacked. Hmm, unless there are two murderers running about in the marina. But that's two murders with the same MO. I need to think." Abigail closed her eyes and held out her hands as if she was moving chess pieces.

Suzie told David, "Don't worry, she always does this. Usually just before she gets a brilliant idea. You just wait, she's marvellous."

Abigail suddenly sat up. "I might not know it all yet, Suzie, but I know why you were killed, David. You were killed because of what you saw."

"What? What did I see?"

"I know exactly what you saw, but I'm not going to tell you yet," said Abigail. "Sorry, but I want to have all my whatsits in a row. What's the saying, Betty?"

"Eggs?" she said hopefully.

"Near enough. Before I have all my eggs in a row, I need to find out one more thing, with the help of Hayley and Tom."

Chapter 20

By the time Abigail and Hayley returned, David MacIntosh had gone. Or given up the ghost, as Betty had joked. In actual fact, he had gone to visit his parents to see how they were on the day when they would be told the worst news of their lives.

"Sorry we've been so long, everybody. Things take twice as long when you're dead."

Terry said, "No worries, but sorry, your boyfriend, David, won't be here for the big denouement."

Betty giggled. "If he was here, we could have had a denudement."

"Oh. Et tu, Betty? Then fall Terry. I really could do with another bloke here. But not him. I couldn't take to him at all."

Abigail shook her finger at him. "Oh, Terry. It's so unfair to say he can't join us just because of how he looks. Live and let live, that's what I say. He seems a perfectly nice…"

"He said you were a meddling, overbearing harpy."

Abigail paused. "That's it, he's banned. I am not a harpy. You're quite right, Terry. He wouldn't fit in with us at all." Terry and Betty looked at each other and smiled. "You're more than enough man for us. Now shall I start?"

"Do you know it all now?"

"I rather think I do, Suzie. So here goes. You'd better all have a seat because this is a complicated affair, which began with the killing of Leo Spencer at the Ottersmill Regatta, and ended with the brutal murder of David MacIntosh. The same MO, but I would say that David's murder was a spur of the moment thing. The murderer had to come out of their comfort zone.

But just for a change, I'm actually going to start in the middle. I think, in a way, Moira's attack was the most important, as it shone a light on the other two that might never have been lit and stayed in the dark. As she told Hayley, she was going to find the killer if it killed her, and it nearly did."

"She didn't actually say that, hun."

"I'm just adding a bit of drama, Hayley. You can use it in the book. And the line about being in the dark. So I think we can discount those who weren't connected to the marina. Noah and Ruth's neighbours, for instance. That leaves Rupert and Ruth, Gail Fletcher, Nina Moore, Ben Manson; they were at the club for the attack on Moira. I daresay even Jack was nearby. And of course, Barry Potts.

You see, he was there for all three attacks and I can't imagine his wife would be that much fun to live with. But he had an alibi for Leo, you're saying. Yes, he did. But he might have wanted to strangle her for years and just timed it to look like it was connected to Leo's murder because he had a rock-solid alibi. The police would just think it was done by the same person as the first one and he'd be off the hook and rid of his wife."

Suzie said in awe, "See what I mean, she's so clever. We would never have thought of that. So is that what happened?"

"Er, no. But it could have. And if David hadn't been killed he would have been very high on my list as well. Very handy to have a reason to be on the spot to help Moira if he had just throttled her. So now we have to work out what David actually saw?"

Lillian said, "He must have seen Moira's attacker going in or coming out of the gate. Or if not that, they were running away and just assumed that they'd been seen by him when he hadn't, but they couldn't chance it. Anyone of them could have crept out the back door, attacked Moira, and then gone around to the front and in the club again."

"Actually, that is a good point. I hadn't thought of that. But I have a feeling that I'm right. What David saw was what got him killed."

Terry sighed and said, "Yes, we know that, but what did he see?"

"I'll tell you exactly what he saw," said Abigail, pausing for effect. The others all looked puzzled and begged her to explain.

"Don't keep us in suspenders, dear," said Betty.

"Alright, I'll tell you. David saw nothing. Absolutely nothing. He didn't see anyone going in the gate and he didn't see anyone coming out of the gate. And there was no one going up the lane. He told us that himself."

"So that proves that someone from inside the bar went out there, attacked her, and went back in again. So how do you know which one?"

Abigail paused and smiled. "So why was the gate open? There was only one person that could have wanted it open."

Hayley was the first to catch on. "I see. David didn't see anything at all. He was in the wrong place at the wrong time. So did David open the gate?"

"No. There was only one person that wanted it open and told everyone that it was."

"Moira Potts said it was open. Moira opened the gate herself?"

"Exactly, Hayley. You've got it."

The others looked puzzled. "So you're saying. Actually, what are you saying?" asked Lillian.

"Moira killed Leo, Moira attacked herself. And Moira killed David."

Chapter 21

TERRY GRIMACED. "MOIRA? BUT ARE YOU FORGETTING that she was working in the bar when the regatta was on? And the only time she left was when someone told her that a girl had been sick in the toilets, and she went to clean it up. She wouldn't have had time."

"Surely you've learned by now not to believe everything you're told, Terry. She said that someone had come to the bar and told her that, so she got the mop and bucket from the kitchen and off she went. How easy is it to say to her husband, 'I've just been told there's a mess I've got to clean up'? I bet if they really checked, she got that pretend message just before three o'clock when she had arranged to meet Leo. It said he was going to meet her on his calendar."

"It said NP, not MP," said Lillian. She was sure that she had caught her out at last. Much as she admired her, she was a bit arrogant.

"I know. But Nina was called LN - Little Ninny. So who is NP? We saw Kia written a few times on his calendar as well. But even that, correct me if I'm wrong, Lillian…"

"Don't worry, I will."

"Even that was written in capitals. So I got to wondering if that was a nickname as well as LN for Little Ninny. Ruth told the police she didn't know a Kia. It actually read, 'Get dates off KIA'. Now who would have had dates of something that he needed. All his business dealings were on his laptop and there was no KIA on there. So it must be something to do with him being commodore. I'm only guessing, but it could be Gail Fletcher or most likely Ben Manson. It doesn't really matter, but I'm guessing it could stand for Know-It-All. So what could Leo's name be for Moira, knowing what we do about her?"

"Nosy Parker!" shouted out Betty.

"She's definitely that," said Hayley. "Not proof though, is it? And I hate to tell you, Abi, she's not left-handed."

"Who better to use her left hand than someone that spends their entire life watching and reading whodunits to confuse the police. I would do that myself I've often thought. She used to row at university, she told you, and may still do. It's one of the few sports that you need to have both your arms as strong as each other. Especially if you do the one with two oars. I was just thinking, I wonder who that F was, that had a phone number written next to it on his desk at the club. I'm guessing that didn't stand for Friend," Abigail joked.

Terry really wanted her to be right about Moira. Annoying as she was, she would be so embarrassed if she was wrong. Also, because once this case was finished they might be able to go somewhere nice while it was still fine weather. "But, Abi, how would she be able to get there in such a short time and no one see her?"

"Hayley should have guessed this. We've even got an eye-witness. Actually, an ear-witness."

"I have no idea what you're talking about, hun."

"We all saw it, and I'm betting you did when we left by the back entrance yesterday. What was opposite the bins? As Lady Caroline said, lots of people have them."

"A bike. Of course, Abi. It was an electric one too. One of their bigger ones. That would have got her there in no time. No wonder the boy didn't see her. She'd have left out the back across the grass and straight to the willow tree. And she would have been out of sight by the time Jacob got there. It can go a lot faster than anyone can run. Brilliant."

"It was too dry for there to be bike tracks on the short grass, but Tom might find some near the lane in the longer grass. And the ear-witness won't be able to give evidence in court, unfortunately."

"They have to by law, hun."

"They'd have a job. He's been dead nearly a hundred years!"

"Willy Morgan?"

"Yes. He heard a whoosh when he saw the newly dead, Leo. Could that have been the bike pulling away on the towpath?"

"Yes, it could. It's not loud, but they do make a bit of a whirring noise. And I bet she went off at speed."

Betty said, "I really believe you, Abigail. But everything you've said is circumcisional."

"That is true, Betty. Well, very nearly true. It is circumstantial, but there might be some proof. I kept thinking I'd seen something important the day of the regatta and then I remembered what it was. Near the body was a shortish piece of rope that forensics took away. Ropes and boats and rivers go together, so not much was thought of it. But that's what we were doing before the meeting. Hayley and I got in touch with Tom and he went and checked if it could be. And it was."

"Was what?" asked Suzie.

"A bit off an old mop, of course. It must have got caught on the wheel or pedal as she put it down and then hopped on the bike. Forensics will tell us for sure. And this is a guess, but I bet she was wearing her rubber gloves. She'd know not to leave fingerprints. But it's hard to kill one person without leaving a trace, let alone two. There could be her DNA on the branch she hit David with. But now they know what to check, I have a feeling that they'll find blood on the left handlebar of the bike. A wound like that would have spurted out on her hand for sure. We'll have to ask Barry if she ever put on an apron for when she cleaned. What was she wearing that day, Betty?"

"I did notice because I thought it was rather nice. A red and black flowery dress."

"Very good for hiding blood splatter, I would think. I don't know if she always meant to implicate Rupert, but that worked out well for her. Or was it because he became a suspect when he was found with Ruth? We'll probably only find out if she confesses."

Lillian asked, "But Moira was attacked. I couldn't check it myself, but you said there were marks on her neck."

"She must have already put the rope out there, or it was in her rubbish she was taking out. Then all she had to do was make a few scratches at the front of her neck, and put the rope round her throat, cross over the ends at the back and pull hard. Moving it from side to side would make even more of a mark. Then she opened the gate, lay on the floor, pulled at the rope to the point of passing out, and started shouting and screaming for help. They were still questioning everyone, so she needed to make sure they arrested Rupert. Maybe someone had started to suspect her. Murderers get very paranoid, and don't forget she had a very nosy woman ask her all sorts of questions. Yes, you, Hayley. Perhaps she was timing the attack on herself for when she saw Rupert outside and then put the plan into action then. I think she was rather enjoying it as well. She liked to mix things up."

Lillian said, "That is feasible. So we have the means and the opportunity, but what was the motive for killing Leo? Or don't you know?"

"Of course she knows. Don't you, Abigail?" said Suzie, not altogether convinced of the answer.

"Of course, Suzie. I think."

Betty asked the next question. "So was the murder to do with whatever was going on at the marina? Or was Moira in love with him? Maybe she didn't know that he had finished with Nina."

"No, nothing to do with love at all, or even the marina, as it happens. It was all to do with bikes, Betty. Diane Parry said that one of the reasons that Leo and Ruth married was so that Leo got the money to start up his business. She said he asked all his friends and family for help. And Moira and Leo had both grown up locally.

And it's not just money when you start out. There's the marketing, sourcing the goods, the website and how to get orders and do the advertising. Now, who do we know, Hayley, that has got a business degree from university?"

"Moira," they all shouted.

"I wonder how much he promised her. A percentage or maybe a lump sum when he got successful. I don't think for a moment Moira would think he would become a multi-millionaire. And friends don't bother with contracts."

"In my day, a handshake was enough," said Terry.

"Moira believed that too. So when she had had enough of Barry, I think she asked him for some money to leave and start somewhere else. She knew he could afford it. But he must have turned her down. Maybe offered her a few thousand, but that was it. She deserved more, I reckon. Noah could tell us how much she had given him.

Then I think the final nail was hammered home. He got another dream that she'd prayed for."

Suzie asked, "Was it the love of Nina?"

"No, she didn't care about that. No, Leo was going to be a father. Ruth was pregnant," as everyone gasped.

"How wonderful," said Hayley. She didn't want to say that she had already guessed. "After what she went through, that is beautiful. Moira did say she wanted a family and that would mean they would have to move out of the flat. Was it Rupert's? But how can you know all that? We've had the same info."

"Three things. Remember the letter from the doctor? It said something about the news and that she shouldn't do this alone. Then Nina said Leo broke it off when he saw something, and then he looked happy with Ruth on Sunday. After Willy Morgan heard him say, 'It's mine', that gave me an inkling. So me and Suzie went to check her rubbish bin."

"Is that what that was?" said Suzie. "A pregnancy test? And Leo saw it in the bin or somewhere in the house. I'm so stupid. That makes much more sense. When I saw it in the bin I thought it was a thermometer like Mummy used to put in my mouth. Before she got the one that went in your ear."

"Actually, I saw five in there, so she wasn't taking any chances of it being wrong," said Abigail. "She wouldn't have been able to take the disappointment. It must be early days, so I'm not surprised she didn't tell everyone."

"So what did Willy say? I missed that," asked Suzie.

"He said Leo was happy when he died and said, 'It's mine'. I couldn't think what else it could be. It wasn't said like it was his money, so get lost. And Willy thought he sounded happy about it. If Moira was the one that told Leo there and then, she must have eavesdropped on Ruth and Rupert in the club when she told him the good news. I can only think that she heard Rupert say that it couldn't be his. So therefore it was Leo's. They still shared the same bed."

"Moira didn't miss much of what was going on in that place, she told me that. And then to tell him he's the father and then take it all away is awful. I think out of all of our murderers she is the most evil. Tom said that Rupert had grown-up children, so perhaps he'd had a vasectomy. I'll get Tom to check."

"Oh, I'm sure the scar will still be there," said Betty.

Hayley laughed. "I was rather thinking he would just check his medical records."

"That would probably be easier," agreed Betty with a grin.

"So Moira Potts could be undone by a mop. The Case of the Old Mop," said Terry.

"I prefer The Case of the Deadly Regatta," said Abigail. "The only thing that worries me is that Johnson is going to go crazy when he hears all the ideas have come from Tom."

"He should be at least a sergeant by now," said Lillian.

"Not while Johnson is head of CID. He's going to get such a shock later. I almost feel sorry for him."

"Nah," they all said together.

Chapter 22

WHILE ABIGAIL HAD BEEN TELLING THE OTHERS WHO the real culprit was, DCI Tony Johnson and Sergeant Dave Mills were sitting across the table from Rupert Cox KC and his own lawyer, Marcus Bentley-Snod. He had been read his rights and been kept in a police cell overnight.

"Feels like old times, sir. I knew you'd be back here the minute I set eyes on you. How's Mrs Cox?"

"I think you know. She kicked me out. That's why I'm living on my boat at present."

"Handy for you when you attacked Moira Potts."

The lawyer jumped in. "You have no proof of that."

"We will have soon. You lied when you said you were on your boat. That's enough to arrest you. Jack Smith saw you by the shop."

"Chandlery," said Rupert as he rolled his eyes.

"Whether you were by the shop or the chandlery, you were lying."

"Why would I want to kill Moira? I only spoke to her when I ordered a drink."

"She was getting close to naming you. Or was it because you heard Moira say that she'd seen you the day of Leo's murder? She'd already told us that you didn't meet up with Ruth until nearly half past three. Is that why you cut a bit off your rope and waited until Moira came out?"

"I'm a barrister, as if I'd be stupid enough to use my own rope."

"Stupid enough to lie."

"And how would I know when she would be going out the back?"

"You've maybe seen her routine."

"Look, Inspector, you've had my client here for nearly twenty-four hours now."

"I know the drill. We've got a strong case all ready for the CPS," he said smugly. "And for the murder of Leo Spencer."

"I've heard that there has been another murder at the marina. Surely that exonerates my client."

"Not at all. That could be part of his plan. We'll need to check where Ruth Spencer was last night. She was hoping to clear her boyfriend, more than likely. I always thought the two of them might have killed her husband," said Johnson.

"On that matter, my client has some additional information that you might not know about Ruth Spencer."

"Go on then. But it won't make me change my mind."

Rupert squirmed in his seat. "Ruth was pregnant, Inspector. And it wasn't mine."

"If it was her husband's, that has just given you another motive. Thank you, Mr Cox. So you killed him in a jealous rage. Oh yes, all the evidence points to you, sir."

Karma could not have timed it better. There was a knock at the door and a worried-looking Tom Bennett said, "Could I have a word with you and Sergeant Mills, sir? Some new evidence has come to light!"

Not long after the interruption, Rupert was returned to his

cell. He had no idea why, but noticed Johnson was slightly more friendly to him when they returned after that nice police constable had walked in on the interrogation.

He couldn't believe this was happening to him. He was very fond of Ruth, maybe even loved her, but he wouldn't have risked his career and freedom for her. He didn't even want her to get a divorce. He would never marry again; Esther had put him off marriage for life. Since the children had left home, he'd had more time to spend on his boat and she had her own interests. It might not be another man, but how many times did she have to stay in London for shows? Maybe he was the naive one.

He couldn't tell anyone that Ruth had broken off their arrangement on the day Leo was killed. That could be seen as another motive. Things hadn't been the same since Ruth had brought up the subject of him having another child with her. She'd gone very quiet when he'd said that his three were enough and anyway he'd had a vasectomy. He understood her disappointment after she had said that she was pregnant. So they had arranged to meet on Sunday, at her instigation, and that was when she had told him that it would be their last meeting.

It did make him wonder if she had killed Leo and was trying to frame him. Maybe so her husband could never get custody of their baby. But he couldn't believe that of her. She never talked about her past, but he always had the feeling that something had happened to her when she was younger. Something so sad that she couldn't even tell him. She wouldn't be the type to make anyone else feel that way. Not him and definitely not Leo.

Rupert had spent his life serving justice to others, but now was starting to lose faith in the system. If he got out of this he would always be more sympathetic to those who said they were innocent.

He laid back on the hard bed and longed for the king-size one in his house. Even the bunk on board the boat was softer than this. If he was released, and he had a feeling that he would be, he decided to make it up with Esther, if she would have him back. They'd already celebrated twenty-five years; they could make it work. Sell the boat and move away. He smiled for the first time in days.

Chapter 23

LESS THAN THREE DAYS LATER, MOIRA POTTS WAS LED from the cell that Rupert had been held in, into the interrogation room. The only difference was that Moira had a far less qualified lawyer, a young woman called Ms Laura Anders. So far she had advised her client to say nothing in the interview, which hadn't helped Johnson's temper.

"I knew you were trouble the minute I saw you."

"So you arrested Rupert," Moira said sarcastically.

"Just gathering the evidence. Once I'd worked out you were guilty it was as easy as sin. For the tape, I'm showing Mrs Potts a photograph of an electric bike. Is this your bike?"

"It could be. We have one similar, but there's a lot of them about these days."

"It's covered in yours and your husband's fingerprints so I'm guessing it is."

"So why even ask?"

Johnson ignored her. "That's not the only thing, Mrs Potts. How do you think traces of Leo Spencer's blood, group A, were found in the grooves of the rubber on the left handlebar?"

"He must have used it at one point and cut his hand. You'll have a job to prove he didn't."

"Your husband denies Leo ever went anywhere near it. But say he did, you might have a harder job to explain how his blood was found on a black and red dress that you had tried to wash. And your DNA was also found on the branch that killed David MacIntosh. You got sloppy, Moira. You're not clever enough to be a murderer. You might have got away with one, but not two. Is that why you killed Leo Spencer? He had brains," Johnson goaded. "He was a great bloke. Everyone loved him. He was good-looking, successful. And he had a brilliant head for business, didn't he? Do you know his company is worth three million? And he started it all from nothing."

Moira's eyes darkened. "A great businessman? You must be joking. He didn't even know what to do first. I did everything. Even the name, Estryke, was my idea. He wanted to call it Spencer's Cycles. I mean, come on. He just had the idea of selling the odd bike online. It was me that said we should build a brand. Be selective where we sell them and go for quality parts and batteries, and make sure the customer service was better than any other company's. He was a joke."

Her lawyer tried to stop her rant. "Moira, you don't have to say anything. Let me do the talking."

"Bit late for that. I hated Leo. He wasn't nice." Moira slumped in her chair. "I gave him everything I had at the time. Barry had spent most of my money by then, but I had two thousand pounds that I'd got hidden away. And I worked day and night on the business plan and website. He promised me ten per cent or a lump sum once the business had taken off. But there was always an excuse. They needed more stock. They were going to expand. About a month ago, I said I'd had enough, I was leaving Barry. He offered me six thousand pounds. Said I was lucky. Not many investments tripled your money. He denied saying I could have ten per cent and asked if I was crazy. I think he found out I was. He even had the nerve to say I'd never paid him for the bike he gave me. Huh, bet he wishes he hadn't given me it now."

"Word is, it wasn't the only reason you wanted him dead."

"That was jealousy. If I couldn't have the career and money, I wanted a family. If I fell pregnant we would have had to move out of that flat then. But no, he even had to get that too. I heard Rupert and Ruth talking in the bar on Thursday. They were talking about children and he said he'd had a vasectomy. I could tell by her face and the way that she had her hand on her belly that she was having a baby. So it had to be Leo's. When I heard that he'd dumped love-struck Nina, I knew he'd found out. Ruth hadn't told him yet. I'm guessing even if it was Rupert's, he didn't care. So on the Friday I asked him again if I could have what I needed to leave Barry and he said no. Said he needed it even more now, but of course he didn't say why."

"So what happened on the riverbank?"

"I caught him when he left for home on Saturday, and I told him I absolutely had to meet him at three o'clock the next day. I made it sound like life or death and his curiosity made him come, I guess. So I did what any good friend would have done. I told him the good news that Ruth was pregnant and it was his baby. Then I hit him."

"Did you mean to kill him?"

"Of course. He owed me, so I owed him."

"Why frame Rupert?" asked Mills.

"He was always splashing the cash, and not once did he buy me a drink. Barry, yes. But I was always the invisible one. Working twice as hard and getting ignored. It was my pleasure to serve him up on a platter. Shame it didn't work."

Mills wanted to know, "Do you feel any guilt for killing David MacIntosh or Leo?"

"David, maybe. But he ignored me too, so not really. I think it was only a matter of time before he realised that it must have been me that opened the gate. After he had got out of his car he had been in view of it for a couple of minutes. Of course there wasn't anyone who had gone in or out. And Leo, not one bit of remorse. I arranged to meet him on Sunday, for something life or death. And it was!"

Chapter 24

As summer was turning into autumn, the members of The Deadly Detective Agency were sitting in Hayley's back garden. Lillian and Suzie had gone back to the school to check on Jordan, Camille and Anya. Luna was enjoying playing with his spirit mum, Tiggy, while the others all sat on the decking discussing the case.

Moira had been arrested at six o'clock in the morning on the previous day. Barry tried to stop them, not believing for a minute that his wife was capable of such a thing. He promised to get a lawyer for her, but the smile she had on her face as she was handcuffed showed her true personality. He looked into her eyes that he'd always said were green, but at that moment looked as dark as her heart. And somehow he knew. He knew Moira was capable. He knew Moira was a murderer, and he knew she hated him.

Betty was the most excited to ask, "What did Johnson say? I bet he was madder than a hatter in March."

"You could say that. He almost hyperventilated, Mills said. Especially when he had to apologise to Rupert Cox, who threatened to take him for everything he's got. Although, Johnson did say it was a bit too late for that as his wife had beaten him to it. He was summoned to see the Chief Constable and that can't have been easy for him either. The only thing that saved his job was because he hadn't given a press conference yet. Imagine if he had to backtrack again. Tom said Johnson intended to take the credit and say that it was on his request that he got the uniforms to collect the bike for forensics to look for any blood. He said he wanted to make sure that he had the right man."

"Well, he's never had the right man yet," said Abigail.

"I don't think I'd have wanted to be in Moira's shoes when he questioned her," said Terry.

"I'm sure she was a match for him, hun. She's seen off worse than Johnson. Tom thinks she'll plead guilty, so that will save all the awkward questions at trial for him. It couldn't have worked out better. I think her husband would have met with an accident before long. She seemed to be getting a taste for murder.

But let's forget her for a while, I've got a new mystery that is right up your street, Abigail. I haven't told you the latest about that missing dog. I had a good chat last night with a Barbara Plunket. She was going to her daughter's wedding in North Wales, so she couldn't take Bertie, the West Highland Terrier with her, so she put him into King's Kennels."

"We used to put our dogs in there. Never had any trouble, but it wasn't cheap," said Betty.

"So Bertie was there for five nights, and they picked him up on the Wednesday. But they noticed something strange almost straight away. They'd had him for ten years and knew all his ways, and this wasn't him. This one was loving, obedient, could do all the tricks and was perfect in every way, but wasn't Bertie. They thought about keeping quiet, but decided it wouldn't be fair on the poor people that had picked up a grumpy, snappy Bertie. And if they were honest, it was part of why they loved him. There was only one Bertie."

"Surely that's no great mystery. There must have been another West Highland dog there, and they got mixed up."

"That's the mystery, Betty. They rang up Mrs King, and she checked the books, and there hasn't been a Westie, as she called them, there for months. She appreciated that it could happen as they are always white and generally look pretty similar. But she had no idea where it could have come from."

"Hmm. That is a conundrum. The case of the two Berties. Did he have the right collar on?" asked Abigail.

"His normal brown leather one. But they are very common."

"We'll have to check out the kennels. As you know them, Betty, me and you can go," said Abigail.

Hayley said, "Hang on, I haven't finished yet. I got another email last night. This one is even more exciting. It's from Adreena Van Derson. Have any of you heard of her?"

Abigail touched her chin. "Only the heiress. You surely can't mean her."

"I surely can, hun. The one and only. The Deadly Detective Agency has hit the big time."

Terry had never heard of her. "What are they rich for? Oil, electrics?"

"Luna and Tiggy would know this; pet food and medicines," said Hayley. "As poor as people can get, they always spend money on their animals."

"What does she need us for? She must have a whole team of people she could go to," said Abigail.

"Apparently not. She says she can't trust anyone in her immediate circle, and when she saw our advert in the Chiltern Weekly, she knew she had to get in touch. She wants us to meet her later on today at the Winston Hotel."

"Sorry, Betty, you're on your own. Forget the kennels. I'm going to the five-star hotel," said Abigail.

"Charming. You know what they say, 'Wisdom is better than wealth.'"

"They lied," laughed Abigail.

"I was hoping that Abigail would come with me and you and Terry could go to see about Bertie," said Hayley.

"I'd rather go to the hotel, thank you."

"I'm sorry, Terry. It's just that Abigail will probably be able to work out what's going on quicker than us. Obviously she's only going as an observer. Promise, Abigail?"

"Cross my heart and hope to die. Oh sorry, I already have. Of course, I'll just observe. And Terry, we could go to the Winston for a romantic date one night. Maybe the weekend if you're really lucky."

"I suppose I can wait. But why do I get the dog kennels and you get the posh hotel?"

"It is advertised as a five-star kennel," said Betty.

"Hmm. Not quite the same. Okay, I've been going to the dogs for years. So what's the matter with this Van Derson woman?"

"She says someone is either trying to send her crazy or kill her."

"Really. How much are we going to charge her?"

"I have no idea, Terry. I suppose it depends on how successful we are. I won't charge Mrs Plunket so much. It's alright for you, Abigail, you don't have to get changed, but I don't think I've got anything posh enough to wear for the Winston."

"Just be yourself," said Betty. "You're perfect the way you are."

Hayley didn't feel much like Hayley Moon when she parked in the underground car park of the Winston Hotel. Whatever Betty thought, she didn't feel the right fit for a meeting with a billionaire. She had found a navy skirt and a navy jacket that was practically the same colour, and her hair had been pinned up by

Suzie in what Abigail had told her was a chignon. Although Hayley was convinced that that was something out of Star Trek.

Hayley, accompanied by the unseen Abigail, entered the art deco Tulip Lounge and saw two ladies who looked the right age. Only one of them raised her hand and beckoned her over. Adreena Van Derson was not beautiful, Hayley thought, but handsome. Her chestnut hair was cut immaculately in a long bob, and the clothes and make-up were similarly faultless.

"I recognised you from the website. But you look a lot younger on that."

Abigail stifled a laugh. "Hi. I'm Hayley Moon."

"Adreena Van Derson. Sit down, please. Can I get you a drink?"

"Just a decaf coffee, please."

"Waiter. Decaf coffee for my guest."

Hayley got her pen and pad out to look more efficient and wondered why her heart was pounding. She'd never felt like this when she met clients for a reading. She felt a bit of a fraud posing as a detective, even if she had been doing it for a while. She tried to take it all in as Adreena told her about all the strange things that had been plaguing her.

"So, Hayley, do you think you can help me? If you're wondering why I don't go to the police, it's not so easy when you're a billionaire. People treat you differently, and if the press got hold of it, it would be all over the papers and the internet. And I have absolutely no proof of any of this. I'd be a laughing stock. But I'm sure that someone is trying to send me insane, scare me to death, and now I know that someone is trying to kill me. Because yesterday morning something tangible happened. I'd bought my cousin's children some toy cars and someone had placed them on the top step so I would fall. And it nearly worked."

"Could it be the kids just playing around?"

"I did check just in case, but they denied it, and I believe them. I'm at a loss to explain it. If it wasn't for everything else, I probably wouldn't have taken much notice. Tell me what you think is happening."

"Yes, it could be paranormal, but it could also be a human hand. Things like the car keys being moved could be someone playing tricks, and even the lights going off could be done if someone knew about electrics. The footsteps are a bit harder to account for. Although that could be a recording being played. Did it come on suddenly in Brighton? If it's an old building, then I'm sure there would have been activity there before. Maybe we could find out."

"I spoke to the estate agent, and they had never had any complaints before, and neither had the neighbours."

"Hmm. Even then, why would it carry on in the London flat? And you say the same kind of thing is happening down here? If it is paranormal, it could be you have a negative entity that's being drawn to you. If not, you've got a very powerful enemy. I'm not sure which is more dangerous. Haven't you got any friends or boyfriends you could go to?"

"I'm engaged to a financial advisor, Lewis Kemish. But he works away a lot. To be honest, I'm not sure if we're even going to get married. He wants to as soon as possible, but I'm in no hurry."

"Could it be him? Trying to scare you so you name the day? He's got a billion reasons," said Hayley, wondering if she had said too much.

"That is always at the back of your mind when you come from money. Sometimes I envy people as poor as you."

Hayley was slightly offended but carried on. "So tell me about your cousin."

"Viktor? My father left him Luxborough Grange in his will. My mother passed away when I was ten. Daddy died there a few months ago in an accident. I didn't mind that Viktor and Harriet had inherited it. I already knew the terms of his will, so I wasn't shocked or anything. They're a lovely couple. We have two more country homes, in Cumbria and Norfolk. I only chose to come to Becklesfield because it's noisy as his family lives there, and there's always plenty of servants moving about. You're lucky if you get any peace."

Abigail urged Hayley to ask about her father's death. "Did you say your father had died there? Does that worry you? Was his death definitely an accident?"

"Of course. Else I would have asked you to investigate that. He did fall down the stairs himself, but there was nothing suspicious about it. He wasn't in the best of health at the time. And if you're thinking it's Daddy's ghost, he would never hurt me. And ghosts don't set traps to send you flying down a flight of stairs."

"She'd be surprised," Abigail said out loud to Hayley.

"Could someone be trying to kill you for your money? What happens to it if you die?"

"It's stipulated that it is shared out between the remaining family. Which would be Viktor and my brother, Casper. My father made sure of that. I own half the business, but Casper became the CEO. If I was married, any money I had would go to Lewis."

"So he wouldn't want you to die before you were married. Although he might be wanting to speed things up. What about the servants?"

"My father only left the butler and housekeeper two hundred pounds each, and they'd been with him for years. So I doubt they were expecting much from me, if anything. There are about three maids and a girl who comes in from the village to help with the heavy cleaning. Then there's various gardeners, and the chauffeur lives over the garage. I was thinking in bed last night, if it could be someone that's seen me in the society pages and started stalking me?"

"We can't rule out anything yet."

"Throughout it all, I haven't seen a ghost, so that proves it's a person doing this to me, and it's all smoke and mirrors. I know it says on your website that you're a psychic medium and all that rubbish as well, but I don't believe in that. Although I was starting to the other night, so I'm hedging my bets, as it were."

Hayley blew out her cheeks. "Well, I'm slightly offended if I'm honest. It could be paranormal, but actually, I agree with you after what you've told me."

"Well, do your best. But I won't be paying if you don't get results."

Hayley bristled. "Detective agencies don't work like that, Adreena. It will be two hundred a day plus expenses. Take it or leave it." Abigail was very impressed at this assertive Hayley.

"Very well, I'll take it. But no bonus until you tell me who's doing it. And there's another clause. No going to the police with what you've learned. Come straight to me, and I'll decide if we tell them. It is my family, after all. If I hear you have, I'll sue you for breach of confidence, and you'll never work again. Now, I've written all the names and addresses et cetera down for you, and I'll expect a daily report on the email I contacted you with."

"All understood. I'll put my best people on it. They're very professional. You won't even know they're there."

"Good, because I've got something special for you to do. I've called in a favour with ExStream Magazine. They owe me. I've told them you're a journalist, and they've given you an introduction to interview my brother, Casper, tomorrow at his house in Mayfair."

"I'm sorry, Adreena, we have our own ways and arrange our own interviews."

"I'm paying you, so I just assumed that you'd follow my wishes. And there's no way my brother would talk to someone like you."

"Er, I have got on okay so far. Even members of the aristocracy have spoken to someone like me," said Hayley, who had started to put her things back in her bag.

"I'm sorry, Hayley. I could have worded that better. I apologise. I mean that it's the only way someone as pig-headed and snobby as my brother would talk to you."

"I see. Alright. I'll see him. Is that it?"

"Nearly. One more little thing that I need you to do for me. I've told the housekeeper, Mrs Barnes, at Luxborough Grange, that my personal maid will be arriving tomorrow afternoon."

"That's a good idea to have …. Oh no, you don't mean me, do you?"

"It will be the perfect cover to be there and meet everyone. Plus stop anyone from actually hurting me. You can sleep in my room. God knows I need a good night's sleep."

"I really don't think I could pull that off."

"Did I mention I'd pay you double the daily rate?"

Hayley thought how much that would mean to Suzie's family and reluctantly agreed but wanted to know what she would have to do.

"Nothing too much. Lay my clothes out, run me a bath, do my hair and fetch and carry. Not much at all. We don't make our staff wear uniforms. But make sure you have on a white blouse with a black, knee-length skirt and black tights and shoes. You're to meet Casper at ten o'clock tomorrow on the dot. He hates tardiness and has probably only scheduled you for thirty minutes. That will give you plenty of time to get to Luxborough at five in the afternoon. And don't forget to go in the back entrance. The staff will be suspicious if you don't. I've written their names down as well, yours is Anna. As regards the interview, your name is Zoe Trent, and you've been with ExStream for a year. You're doing a piece on heirs who take over large firms. Thank you, Hayley. I'll leave you to it then."

Adreena walked out of the bar without so much as a goodbye.

Abigail stood up and watched Adreena Van Derson walk out. "She's not very nice, is she?"

"I don't suppose you have to be when you look like that, and you're an heiress," sighed Hayley.

"True. But it increases the count of people that want you to fly headlong down a flight of stairs. Including me now. What an awful woman."

"Wasn't she, hun. I'll drink my coffee, and then we'll go." Hayley was beginning to get ventriloquist skills as she talked without moving her lips, for the benefit of those who were around her. But Abigail did wonder what a goffee was!

Chapter 25

As Terry and Betty walked into King's Kennels, Kylie Quinn felt a cold breeze and all the dogs began to bark at once.

"It looks exactly the same as when we came. Mrs King ran it then, but now I think she stays more in the house up the hill. This young lady wasn't there. I wonder how much it is now. It was about ten pounds a night then."

"You can triple that, I reckon, Betty. Living in the orphanage, we never had a dog, so I never felt the need to get one."

"We were never without one while the children were about. If one died, we'd get another one straight away. It was like we'd lost a member of the family. It felt strange without one. There are twelve pens here, so they must be making a fortune. Not so much in the winter. But they're fully booked now."

The barking had stopped, but Kylie noticed that a lot of the dogs had retreated to the back of their cages. What had got into them, she wondered. But it made feeding time easier.

Betty looked around. "They all have their collars on and their leads are hanging by their doors. And their names are on each cage as well. It's hard to see how they could have got mixed up.

I know they take them out for walks, but we had a Jack Russell called Jacko that wasn't very friendly with people or other dogs, so they would just open his door and he'd run out into a fenced-off pen and have a runaround and a sniff. Let's have a look out there."

There was a small Cavalier King Charles Spaniel running around. Betty told him as he would never have known.

"So, Betty, if all the cages were full, where did this one come from?"

"Maybe it belongs to her."

The girl joined them and picked it up, but rather than take it back, she locked it in a small shed.

"That is very strange. Do you think she's taking on extras and pocketing the money herself?"

"Looks like it, Terry. So that's how Bertie went to the wrong owner. They must have both been out here. Let's follow her." She walked back and went in the door marked Manager - Kylie Quinn. Her mobile rang and she answered it straight away.

"Hi. How did it go? And they can pay? I'll bring him. Yeah, everything is fine here. See you there. Bye."

"Sounds like they're fiddling on the side to me, Betty. If they're doing it for twenty or thirty a night, they're making a fortune. We can get Hayley to confront her and get her to say who the illegal dog was. Then swap them over. Sorted. Let's get back to the library and tell the others. I wonder if they're back from the hotel yet. Well, we can tell them we've solved our mystery. Abigail will hate that."

"Are you sure we have, though, Terry? It seems too easy to me. I'm not sure they'd be able to get away with hiding dogs in there for more than a few hours. Supposing Mrs King came to see how they were getting on. And I know that when you pick up a dog, you expect it to come out of the pens."

"All I know is that Abigail will soon tell us if we're wrong. It doesn't seem fair that they get a billionaire and we get dogs."

"Give me a dog any day, Terry."

Hayley and Abigail were thinking the same thing as they made their way back to Becklesfield.

Hayley and Abigail had joined everyone in the back of the library and learned what had happened at the kennels and told them what had happened at the hotel.

"Honestly, Betty, she wasn't as nice as you would have thought," said Hayley.

"That's the difference between us. I wouldn't have thought that she was very nice at all. All that money can't do a lot for your personality. But I'm not one to judge. And whatever she is like, it doesn't give someone the right to try to kill her."

"Who have we got on the list so far?" asked Terry.

"It depends if you think it's the living or the dead, hun. I think the living are more murderous myself. Whoever or whatever is messing with her, it started in Brighton. It seems to be getting worse now that she's at her childhood home. So at the moment, the suspects are her cousin, Viktor and his wife, Harriet. One or both had the opportunity to put the cars on the stairs and play tricks on her in the bedroom. They could have paid someone to scare her at the other places. Then there's her brother, Casper. I'm not sure if he's married. And there's a boyfriend, Lewis Kemish. Tell them about her father, Abigail."

"That's another mystery. Now Karl Van Derson fell down the back stairs and died. But she's sure there was nothing dodgy about that. The inquest ruled it an accidental death. The cousin inherited the house, which must be worth millions, so we really should check it out. Even if she doesn't want us to. Adreena thinks it's just a coincidence."

"And you know what they say about coincidences," said Betty.

"No. What, hun?"

"I've no idea, but they must say something."

"I'm with Betty," said Terry. "It sounds very fishy to me. But we're not being paid to investigate that. We've got enough on our plates without doing extra work. There's the dog business to clear up as well."

Betty laughed. "And you make fun of what I say."

"Oh yes. That's funny. I didn't mean to say that."

Abigail said, "I might have an idea about that dog business. I just need to check something. I have a feeling little Bertie will be easy to find, but I think the Van Derson case is a different kettle of... Betty?"

"Eggs?"

"Precisely."

Hayley asked them a question. "Do any of you fancy a trip to London tomorrow?" Of course, they all did, so she had to make the decision herself. "Abigail, has to come. I'm sorry, but I'll need her. Suzie, you've already missed out on so much in your life that you can come. I'm even going to drive around a bit and show you a few of the sights."

Betty said, "I agree. I've been up to London many times, so I'm quite happy to stay behind."

Terry said the same, so Lillian, Suzie, Abigail and Hayley got into the red Mini on the following morning and Hayley set the satnav for W1.

Chapter 26

CASPER VAN DERSON'S MAYFAIR HOUSE WAS LARGER than the Winston Hotel, Hayley and Abigail agreed. Lillian and Suzie waited in the car and Hayley was admitted by a young maid, who, contrary to her instructions, was dressed like an old-fashioned servant, in a white pinafore and cap. Abigail followed behind and just managed to get in Casper's study before the door was shut. The man himself was behind a large desk and exquisitely dressed in a suit, with a matching tie and handkerchief in his top pocket. Hayley was motioned to sit in the chair opposite, and Abigail, not wanting to be left out, sat on the edge of the desk next to him. Hayley raised her eyebrows at this, but she didn't move.

"So, Ms Trent, this is for the December edition of ExStream magazine. Is that right?"

"Yes. Call me Zoe, please, Mr Van Derson." There was no offer to refer to him as Casper. "We're doing a feature on successful sons or daughters who take over the family business. And of course, you're at the top of our list. Thank you so much for agreeing to see me." Hayley got out her phone. "Do you mind if I record the interview? Or I could do it shorthand."

Hayley took out a pen and pad, praying that she wouldn't have to pretend to do squiggles and lines.

"Recording is fine. It will be quicker I daresay."

"Definitely. So your father was Karl Van Derson of Van Derson Industries. And he died in May, is that correct?"

"I'm sure you already know the answers to those questions, so I suggest for your sake and mine that you ask things that you don't."

Abigail crossed her arms. "What an ar…"

"So let's talk about the company then." said Hayley, while glaring at the side of the desk towards her friend. "How long has it been going and what does it do?"

"Van Dersons is a global specialist in pet pharmaceuticals. We lead the way in diagnostic products, medicines and vaccines. My grandfather had a small vet's practice in the East End of London in the thirties, and then he partnered with a colleague, and Van Dersons & Watermans was born. They were the entrepreneurs of the pet-world, going into animal foods, medicines and all pet accessories. Farms and racing studs all over the world use our products now."

"That is very interesting. What became of Mr Waterson?"

"He died in the sixties. We tried to find any family members, but our solicitors had no joy, so now it's just Van Derson."

Abigail said, "So that could be a lead. Excuse the pun."

"How would you say you've improved the company since you've taken over?"

"I've begun a thorough overhaul of my father's policies. And technology has come a long way, so we need to keep up with our competitors."

"Karl Van Derson made you CEO in the event of his death. Was there any animosity with your sister, Adreena? As a modern woman, did she feel that she should have been made CEO or president?"

"My sister is quite happy spending the money my father left

her. She's never felt the need to work before his death, so I can't think why you would think that she'd want to now."

"I've heard that she is a very intelligent woman. Would you be open to her joining you at the helm?"

Casper started to laugh. "Very intelligent? Is that what your editor told you? Adreena did think that she would get an executive position after his death, but she'd have to do a lot of growing up first."

"No love lost there, Hayl," said Abigail.

"What were you doing at the firm before his death? Were you already high up on the ladder?"

Casper leaned back in his chair. "My father was a hard man, Zoe. He made sure I started right at the bottom, however embarrassing for me. I suppose it has made me more aware of how the business works. I was in accounts in the head office when he died."

"Is there a Mrs Van Derson?"

"My mother passed away when we were young, but I have been married for four years and we have a son."

"So do you all live in Luxborough Grange?"

"No. My father left it to my cousin Viktor for some reason. But we have this townhouse and also our country home in Surrey. It's a lot less drafty than old Lux."

"Have you been there recently? I've heard it's a marvellous sprawling estate."

"Not for a few months. I think the last time was when my father died. I'm not that close to Viktor and Harriet."

Hayley took a deep breath. "Your father's death was deemed an accident. Is there any part of you that thinks that it was suspicious? Or that other members of your family could be at risk?"

"Is that an accusation? That's it, Ms Trent. I don't know what you are trying to say, but I told your editor that I would not take any personal questions of that nature." He pressed a buzzer on his desk and the same maid entered. "Ms Trent is leaving. Please show her out. I will expect a complete transcript of the interview before I allow publication. And that includes any photographs."

Abigail jumped up in a rage. "He really is a little sh…"

"It's just to give our readers a glimpse of the family man behind the firm. To see how he juggles his home life and work after a tragedy."

"I don't juggle and it's none of their business. I'll expect to hear from your editor by next week."

"Of course, Mr Van Derson. Thank you again."

After Hayley and Abigail got in the car, they played the recording for Lillian and Suzie.

"Bit sensitive about his dad's death, isn't he? He could have just said, no, it was an accident," said Lillian.

"And he didn't think much of his cousin or sister. He could easily have arranged to get someone to scare her. Even paid one of the servants to place the cars on the stairs," said Abigail. "We need to check the will. Perhaps there's something in there that worries him. Maybe Adreena could take over her half of the company if she wanted to. And what about Waterson? That's a big reason to bump them off. There could be a long lost heir that doesn't want to share his newly-found inheritance. Maybe Casper is the next victim. We only have his word that there were no Watersons left. They would be entitled to half of the firm and the money, even after all this time. Maybe it's revenge because the Van Dersons stole the company, and the two siblings told the Watersons to get lost."

Hayley agreed. "We can't just believe what he said. Perhaps Adreena can get her solicitors to check. At least it's a lead to share with her."

Suzie couldn't wait any longer. "Pleeease can we get going now? I'm so excited, Hayley."

"I wish I was, hun. I can't believe I'm going to drive around

London. Give me a cellarful of demons any day." Hayley took her life in her hands and pulled into the traffic. She gripped the steering wheel tight and went on Suzie's mystery tour.

The first sight was a drive up The Mall and past Buckingham Palace. The flag was flying, so Lillian explained that it meant that the King was in residence. Hayley was too nervous to take her eyes off the road and look, but she took them safely past Admiralty Arch. Lillian excitedly pointed to the Tower of London and then they made their way to the place that they had all been most excited to see. She knew they were nearly there when they saw a big line of people queuing to get in Madame Tussauds. Hayley slowed down and they all felt a special bond as they stopped outside the small terraced house with the address 221b, Baker Street.

Chapter 27

Hayley had to pull nearly everything out before she found the clothes that Adreena said she had to wear as a maid. At least she didn't have to wear a cap and pinny. Although, Tom would have quite liked that, she thought. Not that he was talking to her at the moment. He was furious that she was going undercover where a murder might be about to happen. He made her promise that at the first sign of danger she would call him and he'd be there with blue lights flashing.

Hayley pulled up at the grand entrance to Luxborough Grange and saw the original gatehouse next to the huge locked gates. In the old days, a gardener or his wife would have opened them for any visitor, but today it was a security guard with a peaked cap and smart uniform, carrying a clipboard. Adreena must have told him that she was expecting her as the gates swung open. He only saw the maid, not the uninvited Abigail and Terry.

The winding drive seemed to be as long as the road that ran through Becklesfield. When they eventually arrived at the grand old house, Hayley turned left by a garage that could house at least four cars. Above it was the flat that Adreena had told her the chauffeur lived in.

"You will be careful, won't you?" said Terry. "This is unknown territory."

"I promise. And I've got a warning for you two. This is an old house, centuries old, so I bet you're not the only ghosts. They might not like you entering their territory and disturbing the balance of things. Any sign of trouble, you get out of there as well."

Abigail said, "If I was alive I'd be scared to death, but they can't do anything, can they?"

Terry said, "I'm not sure. But if they've survived for hundreds of years, they might know a few things. Stay close to me, love."

"Don't worry, I will."

"And we won't call it a date, else something awful is sure to happen."

"Good idea, hun. Now, let's separate to start with. You two can go in the front and do a recce. Plus, I need to concentrate. Let's meet up later when I know what I've got to do. I'm so nervous. I'm sure I'm going to be a hopeless maid. I'm glad it's still summer. Imagine if they said light a fire or lay the table; I wouldn't have a clue. Right, here goes."

Hayley lifted her holdall out of the car and walked to the servant's entrance, where she was surprised to see that it still said 'Servant's Entrance' on an old sign. She banged the brass knocker and waited.

"Hi. I'm Anna, Adreena's maid." That was her first mistake and she hadn't even got in the house yet.

"Miss Van Derson is expecting you," said an even younger maid.

"Come on in," said a friendly voice from the kitchen. "Marcie Brimble, cook."

"Hello. Anna Moon."

"This here is Sarah. She'll take you up to your room. You'll meet Mr Scrivens later. He's on his break again," and she rolled her eyes and went back to her mixing bowl.

They left the vast kitchen and went up the backstairs for four flights. Hayley giggled and said, "I shouldn't be nosy, but is this where old Van Derson died?"

Sarah looked around and said quietly, "Fell down the bit that leads to the kitchen. Broke his neck and smashed his head right in. Scrivens found him the next morning. Mind you, things are much better now. Mr Viktor is a much better boss and Miss Harriet lets us do what we want, as long as the work is done. How long have you worked for Miss Adreena?"

"Only a few months. Mainly in Brighton. She's alright, I guess."

"Cook said she's improved with age, put it that way. So I'm glad I wasn't working here then. Here's your room. It's tiny, but it's bigger than mine."

"That must be small then." There was a bed and a chest of drawers that doubled as a bedside table. An alcove with a curtain was the only place for hanging clothes. It had probably been the same for a hundred years, she thought.

"Leave your bag on the bed and I'll take you to Miss Adreena's suite."

Adreena looked genuinely pleased to see her. "Anna, come in." She grabbed her arm, slamming the door on Sarah, and pulled her to the far side of the room. "Have you found anything out yet?"

"I've only just got here. I've met the cook and Sarah, and they seem really nice. I've yet to meet Scrivens. I can tell you what your brother, Casper, said at the interview. What about you, did anything happen last night?"

"Come with me. I woke up to this." On her bathroom mirror, written in red, was one word - DIE.

"Let's see how the other half live, Terry."

"And hopefully, not die. Why couldn't we have gone somewhere nice, like that hotel?"

"You're kidding. People pay a fortune to stay the night in a haunted house like this these days. It's called ghost-hunting. They come with video cameras and all the equipment."

"What kind of equipment?"

"A little light goes off if a ghost goes near it. And a machine that turns noises into words. Loads of things. Then you send them off to TV shows and they pay them. It's a big thing nowadays."

"Nothing surprises me after you told me about pub quizzes. Pubs were for drinking in my day, and if you wanted to see a ghost you went to the pictures."

"But these are real ghosts, caught on cameras or phones. I didn't always believe it, but now I totally do. And the ghost-hunters always say, 'If there is anybody here, show yourself, or make yourself known.' And if they do, or if they move something, they start screaming. At least we don't have to worry about being terrified."

"Terry, I'm terrified. I'd pee my pants if I could. It's like being locked in The Chamber of Horrors at Madame Tussauds."

So far they'd seen two monks, a cavalier, and a particularly nasty medieval knight, who was brandishing a huge sword. Terry loved it when Abigail grabbed him tight as a line of Roman soldiers filed past them and went through the wall, on which hung an assortment of deadly weapons.

"Don't make eye contact and then they'll hopefully think we're still alive. But feel free to hang on to me. I've got you."

"Why she'd want to move here to feel safe is crazy."

"What you can't see, you can't be scared of."

"You sound like Betty," laughed Abigail. "Let's have a look in some of the rooms. Ooh, nice." They entered a huge room that could well have been a sitting room, or maybe a drawing room. After the wood-panelled walls of the hall, it looked light and airy. The highly patterned fabric on the heavy curtains and furniture was green and yellow. A huge fireplace was the centrepiece of the room, although the vaulted ceiling caught Abigail's eye with its decorative coving and huge chandelier. In one of the high-backed chairs, Harriet was sitting with a book in her hand. She wasn't reading it as she had her eyes firmly fixed on the window. Outside, two small boys were playing cricket with a man, possibly Viktor, they thought. Harriet had a smile on her face. Whether it was the sentiment of seeing Daddy and sons happily playing together, or the fact that she had a rest from the two energetic boys, they weren't sure.

Abigail looked to see what she was reading. "The Body in the Library. Very apt."

"Could have been worse. Could have been Lady Chatterley's Lover."

"Read it yourself, have you, Terry?"

"Course not. Saw the film in the eighties. I never did like reading."

"How ironic that you hang out in a library. Mind you, I haven't read it either. But I know what it's about. I wonder if they have a game-keeper. But give me a good murder."

"You might get one if we don't find some clues. What's in here? Oh wow, this is what you call a library. I wish we could find a friendly ghost. Surely there's someone we can talk to. Let's go and have a look at where her father died on the stairs. Suzie looked it up in the Chiltern Weekly for us. He died instantly apparently. He had on his dressing gown and one of his slippers was at the top, so they thought he'd just tripped. But after what happened to Adreena it makes you wonder."

As they got closer to the stairs that ran from the servant's hall, they heard voices and as they rounded the corner they saw a lady and a young girl in her long nightdress. Abigail didn't need Terry to tell her that they were as dead as they were.

"At last," said the lady. "I thought you'd never get here. I take it you're from The Deadly Detective Agency?"

"We are, but who are you?" asked Abigail.

"This is Agnes, a scullery maid, and I'm Brenda."

Abigail thought that Agnes only looked about ten, but didn't like to say. "I can't believe you were expecting us. I take it you're here to tell us that Karl Van Derson was murdered and you need us to save the life of Adreena."

"Oh no," said Brenda. "I'm here to see that she gets arrested for murder. Adreena killed my brother!"

Chapter 28

ABIGAIL FELT THE NEED TO SIT DOWN WHEN SHE heard the shocking news. Not even she had seen that coming.

"What she didn't know was that Karl had already changed his will to leave the Grange to Viktor and his family," said Brenda. "He thought she didn't appreciate the old building like he did. I think he thought she might turn it into a fancy hotel and golf course. He wanted children running around the grounds again. Let's go to the library. It's more comfortable and we won't be disturbed."

Once they were all settled, Abigail begged her to tell them what was going on, but they had another young ghost join them first. He was a tall thin boy, dressed in a scarlet jacket and waistcoat, with black knee breeches.

"This is James, the footman who was here long before we arrived. What news have you?"

"Adreena is getting dressed for dinner and the other agent is helping her. She's safe as long as she doesn't guess anything."

"How did you know we would be here?" asked Terry. "We didn't know ourselves till yesterday."

"We, what's the word, engineered it. I know my niece all too well. All bullies are cowards and I knew she'd want help. She's got through life paying for what she wants, and she always gets it. James is able to haunt and move things, so he went back to Brighton with her the last time she came here and made it impossible for her to stay there. And the same with the London flat. So it was only a matter of time before she came to Becklesfield. You're well known in these parts. The late cook of Chiltern Hall told our dead cook how you helped them and we took it from there. We managed to plant the idea in Hayley Moon's head to put an advert in the paper, and we made sure Adreena saw it. She couldn't resist getting in touch. Hayley isn't the only psychic; the living can be quite predictable when you have the time to observe them like I have."

"So start at the beginning."

"Well, Adreena was always a little madam. Never wanted to share her toys with her brother or friends. She's five years younger than Casper and was always spoiled. She cried crocodile tears and refused to go to boarding school like all of the Van Derson children and that didn't help. She needed some discipline, as she had her mother and father wrapped around her little finger. My sister-in-law passed and Karl doted on her even more. In the end though, he became a burden to her. Relied on her too much for company. He smothered Adreena and didn't want her to leave home once she had grown up. She had no freedom and I think that's why she's in no hurry to marry Lewis. He only proposed after her father died and she didn't want to go from one man controlling her, to another. He's far too good for her anyway.

But Adreena didn't have the money to do as she pleased, and I think that's when she decided to kill him. She begged him for the property in Brighton, telling him they could stay there and go out sailing together on their yacht that's in the marina. But they never did. I think she wanted it to have an alibi for the night of his murder."

"Tell us about that night," said Abigail.

"The day before the murder she went to Brighton to see a parade that was going on. She knew her father wouldn't want to go with all the crowds there. But this is what no one else knows; no one except James and Agnes here. They heard her on her phone, in the early hours saying to him, 'I've come home, Daddy. It's over between me and Lewis.' She knew he'd be delighted at that. 'I can't face anyone. I'm in the kitchen having some hot milk, could you come down the back stairs without anyone seeing you. I only want to talk to you. I need a daddy hug.' So he came down and when he got to the last flight, she was waiting for him. Adreena's last words to him were, 'Dear Papa, this is going to hurt you a lot more than it hurts me.' And then she pushed him."

"That is one cold-hearted woman. Then I suppose she just left without anyone knowing she'd been here."

"That's correct. She knew the shortcut to the back road across the grounds. I had no idea myself until Agnes came and told me. I spend most of my time in the orangery since I died. We had to wait then until Scrivens found him the next morning. It was awful. He passed straight on, luckily. He would have been heartbroken to know what Adreena had done. His dear wife was there to meet him, so that's my only consolation."

Abigail looked at Terry. "So we need to find some proof and see that your brother gets justice. We can do that. It might take a while, but we work with the police, Brenda."

"That's the trouble. You haven't got long. You've got to work fast to stop the next murder."

"Who's next?" asked Terry.

"We believe she's going to kill Viktor. Luxborough Grange will revert back to her then."

Chapter 29

"So you're telling us that our friend, Hayley, is somewhere in this house with a crazy killer?" said Terry.

"She'll be alright as long as she doesn't suspect Adreena of anything. At the moment, she needs Hayley to find out who is trying to scare her. I think she's hoping Hayley will say it is Viktor, and then she can say it is self-defence when she kills him," answered Brenda.

"But Hayley is psychic, she may have sensed it already. This place is like a prison, how could she get out? We need to warn her. But then if we do and she acts differently, Adreena could kill her," said Abigail. "I feel so responsible. I was the one who said she'd be fine."

James had an idea. "As I said, when I left them, she was helping Adreena to get ready for dinner. We could warn her while the family is eating."

"Good idea. Then she could leave a note saying her nan was ill or something. Come on, Terry, let's go and find her. First let's check they're eating. Show us where the dining room is, please, James."

Adreena looked in the mirror. "Well, for a first attempt my hair doesn't look too bad. But if you're here much longer I'll need to get a hairdresser in."

"I've never done a French pleat. Looks pretty good from the back. Do you want me to stay here or come down to dinner with you?"

"You can stay here and tidy up. Nothing will happen with everyone about."

"Be careful walking down the stairs. I feel there is a connection between you and a staircase. I can't understand why you don't think there was anything suspicious about your father's death. Why don't you want me to look into that? If it is Viktor, he could have killed his uncle to get Luxborough surely."

"But he didn't know he was inheriting it, none of us did."

Hayley caught a flicker in Adreena's eyes. That was wrong, surely. Hayley remembered that she had told her that she knew she wasn't going to get the house in the will, so she wasn't surprised or disappointed. But maybe she didn't know. She got the money, but not the house, or the company. Was that why she didn't want them to look into her father's death? It was Adreena. She felt it in her heart at that moment. Adreena had killed her father. But who was scaring her now? Hayley looked back to Adreena's face in the mirror. She looked different now, like Hayley could see her for the first time as she was. A slyness had appeared. Not sly, evil.

"Ah, I slipped up, didn't I? You know, don't you? How silly of me. I thought I'd been so careful. I had no idea that Daddy had left my wonderful Luxborough to that man." Adreena's hand closed around a long hat pin that was in a pot on her dressing table, and she turned round and stood up to face Hayley. "It's such a shame I have to kill you in self-defence, Hayley. I quite liked you. And now I might never know who is trying to send me mad. It must be Viktor or Harriet. They could get half the company and my fortune then. Or a long lost Waterman that you so kindly found out about for me. Yes, I did kill my father, but unfortunately for you, dead men tell no tales."

They felt a gust of cold air and Abigail shouted, "I wouldn't be too sure of that, you bitch!" as the spirits rushed in. "Hayley, it's her. She did it. Don't let her know you know. She could go for you."

Hayley said, "It's too late, she knows."

Adreena frowned. "Who knows? No one knows, you're on your own. I'll tell everyone you went for me and I had to protect myself from this fake medium who was trying to get money out of me for contacting my poor dead father."

Adreena raised her hand holding the deadly weapon, but she hadn't reckoned on a young footman, who grabbed the hat pin and threw it under the bed. While she stood there in shock, James gave her as hard a push as his slight frame would allow and sent her flying to the ground.

"I don't know how you did that, you witch, but no one will believe you. Everyone knows that Daddy's death was an accident. Now get out of my house. And by the way, you're fired and you were the worst maid I've ever had."

"But I'm a damn good detective, so you'd better watch out, 'cos we're coming back for you."

"There's nothing you can do. Money talks and I'll sue you if you go to the police. Now get out before I call security."

Hayley would have left her bag in her room upstairs, but she realised her keys were in it. So she flew up the stairs and back down to the kitchen in record time.

She shouted out to the surprised cook, "I'm off now. Nice to meet you." Hayley didn't want to say anything to anyone that could put them in danger. They needed to regroup and have a really good think about what to do next. And that had to include Tom. Although the only proof they had was a footman and a scullery maid. Both of whom had been dead for over a hundred years.

Hayley was worried that they wouldn't be able to get out the gate, but the same security guard waved the red Mini through and for the first time the three of them could relax.

"I'm so sorry, Hayley. I can't believe I nearly got you killed."

"It's not your fault, hun. How did I not see what she was really like?"

"According to her aunt, she's been manipulating people all her life. They're worried that she's going after Viktor now."

"She's more than capable. I really saw the evil in her eyes. I wonder if she would have killed me. Mind you, I was planning on whacking her with the carriage clock if you hadn't come to the rescue. I don't think I'll tell Tom the whole story. I'd never hear the last of it. He tried to warn me."

"Well, we won't tell, will we, Terry?"

"Our lips are sealed."

"I know this isn't like me, but would you all stay with me till Tom gets home?"

"Of course, Hayl. Terry can go and fetch the others. Suzie won't let anything happen to you."

"I need to go home and have a stiff drink. Then we have to work out how the hell we are going to get a billionaire locked up for good."

Chapter 30

LILLIAN, SUZIE AND BETTY RUSHED DOWN CHURCH Lane to Hayley's as soon as they heard what their friend had been through. Hayley knew she would have to be more careful in future.

"I really can't think what we can do next. I suppose the first thing is to warn Viktor or Harriet. Perhaps I could ring and say who I am and that I've had a vision that they're in danger."

"I don't think they'd believe it without some sort of proof. And if they did, they would call the police and we, well you, would have a lot of explaining to do," said Abigail.

Lillian said, "Could we send a letter to Adreena and say if anything happens to your cousin, we'll tell the police?"

"That would work, but it won't get justice for her poor father. Perhaps I could have a word with Tom to get them to open the case. But again, we'd need even a bit of proof. They might be able to track the car leaving Brighton and going to the Chiltern Hills and back again, but she could say that she was just popping in to collect something. There could be a witness that saw her car parked down the road at the time of death, but she's a billionaire for goodness sake. She can afford the best lawyers and the Chief Constable won't go forward unless there's absolutely no doubt that she did it. He wouldn't want a powerful enemy like that."

Abigail nodded. "Hmm. I wonder if they checked Karl's phone to see if there was a call from Adreena that night."

"That's not a crime. She can phone her own father. I don't know what we can do to stop her, hun."

Betty smiled and said, "I have a brilliant idea," which didn't fill the gang with the greatest of hope.

"No, seriously. Don't laugh. This is what Jessica Fletcher did on one of her investigations, trust me."

Adreena had left Luxborough Grange soon after Hayley had roared down the drive as fast as her small car could go. She had to get away as well, so she phoned the Winston Hotel and booked a suite for that night. Then she rang for Scrivens and told him to get someone to bring a car round to the front for her. She didn't care which one. Half an hour later she had checked into her large room and locked the door behind her. Then, as an afterthought, she pulled over one of the heavy burgundy armchairs in front of it, and then she was satisfied that no one could get to her.

She knew she wouldn't sleep well, not because of her tormentor, but more the fact that Hayley had realised that it was her that had killed her father. She could tell by the way she had looked at her. She had slipped up when she said she didn't know about the will leaving her house to Viktor. Damn him, how could her father have done that to her? It was her family home. Her father had controlled her life and he was still doing it. Her mother was the same. She had tried to send her away from her beloved Lux, to a boarding school in Norfolk, and had put her name down to start as soon as she had turned eleven. Daddy didn't even know until she bought the uniform. That wasn't going to happen. So Mummy had to die. Daddy always thought Casper was the clever one, that was why he had made him head of the company, but she was much more resourceful. Hadn't she noticed that all those capsules Mummy took for her nerves were half-empty? It was easy to fill them right up until she overdosed, or so they thought. The little bit of tablets she crushed in her coffee every day helped as well. Not to mention, she sometimes put a bit of bleach in her dinner when she had annoyed her that day. Adreena smiled at herself in the dressing table mirror. Oh yes, she would be far better at running Van Derson Industries. Any trouble from that Hayley and she would come up with a plan for her as well.

It was just after she woke the next morning that she received a text on her phone from an unknown number. Adreena reread it three times. Someone must have seen her that night on the back stairs. Someone knew her last words to her father were, "Dear Papa, this is going to hurt you a lot more than it hurts me."

And whoever it was wanted her to meet that night at Little Billings Cricket Pavilion and give them fifty thousand pounds. That would never happen. Could it be one of the servants? Sarah was always listening at doors. Although, she bet it was Marcie. Or Mrs Barnes. Not Scrivens. But it could even be Harriet. Viktor kept a tight hold of the money, so this could be her way of sending her crazy and then getting some money of her own, she thought. "But she won't be getting any off me."

Adreena reached for her designer bag and felt the lining. Good, it was still there. The best thing her father had done for her. He always worried about the danger of her being kidnapped, or worse. So he'd given her a small semi-automatic pistol for her eighteenth birthday. She had even thought about using it on him; an accident again, of course, but decided against it. But it would be perfect for the rendezvous tonight at the cricket pavilion. Whoever arrived, she could quite legitimately shoot them. She had a witness that she was being harassed. Hayley would have to tell the truth that someone had tried to kill her and they'd never believe that she was guilty of killing her darling father. She might get in trouble for the gun, but she'd get away with self-defence. Daddy's solicitors could have got Dr Crippen off. Actually, it was rather fun. She hadn't enjoyed anything so much since she'd poisoned Mummy or she'd pushed Daddy to his death. Money couldn't buy that kind of excitement. Feeling happy once again, she rang for room service and ordered a full English breakfast.

Chapter 31

ADREENA SLOWED DOWN AND STOPPED ON THE deserted lane. She had watched cricket here many times with her father and Casper when she was a young girl. She had been bored to tears at the endless waste of time. The only good thing about it was the sandwiches and homemade cakes. It had to be the slowest game in the world, but everyone else there seemed to love it. Even fishing in Scotland had been slightly more exciting, and she had enjoyed killing the fish that she had caught. But it just shows how your life is all planned; as how else would she have known where to go for the meeting? This way there would be no trace on her sat nav if she was caught. Not that she would be; the gun had been from a friend of Daddy's in America, so the bullet could never be traced back to her.

The hours of daylight were shortening, so it was nearly dark by nine o'clock. She couldn't see another car and so she expected it to be one of the servants. They didn't get paid enough to have their own transport. Adreena had taken the small pistol from her bag and put it into her pocket, where her right hand was resting gently on it. In her left hand was her holdall. No longer containing her clothes, but two towels from her hotel room. Did they really think she would give them fifty thousand pounds? As if that would be the last time either.

The automatic light on the front of the pavilion clicked on as she got closer, making her jump when she saw the silhouette of a figure standing on the right.

"I've got your money," said Adreena, as the person stepped forward into the light and surprised her. "You? How could you possibly know what I said?"

Hayley shrugged. "Remember when you said you didn't believe in that rubbish? Turns out you should have. There was a witness there."

"I still think it's rubbish. I bet it was Sarah who told you."

"No. Someone else was there when you pushed your poor father down the stairs, after you lured him down to the kitchen. Especially cruel as you told him you needed a daddy hug. But I can understand it. You wanted your freedom and money. Like me. I can get a lot of freedom for fifty thousand pounds. Let's say every three months. I don't want to be greedy."

"You can't possibly think I'd let a fraud like you blackmail me. I didn't plan his death to perfection for you to ruin everything. My mother tried to cross me and that didn't end so well for her either. You don't know how powerful I am. I take it you're recording this as well." Adreena pulled out her pistol and walked closer to Hayley. "Give it to me and I might let you live."

"Give me the gun and things might go easier for you."

As Adreena laughed she raised her hand to pull the trigger, but two things happened. Suzie knocked the gun up in the air as it fired and Tom and Dave Mills threw themselves at the shocked Adreena. She was thrown to the ground and her hands were handcuffed behind her back.

Tom grabbed Hayley by her arms. "Are you okay? Are you hurt?"

"No, I'm fine. Just feel like I'm about to have a heart attack, that's all."

"Thank God. Where did the gun go?"

"Over there," said Dave. "Good job she's a lousy shot."

"It was almost like someone knocked it out of her hand," said Tom, looking around suspiciously. "So thank you for that."

"Tell me you got it all on tape."

"Yes, of course," said Sergeant Mills. "I'll call for back-up."

"If you're a police officer, you should know that this woman has been harassing me for days. First of all, she stalked me at the Winston Hotel and then she pretended to be a maid, under a false name, and came to our family estate until I threw her out. Not only that, she's a crazy woman who thinks she can talk to ghosts. She sent me a text to blackmail me and made up some story about me having killed my father. I brought my gun as I feared for my life. She's a mad woman, officer. You don't know what she's like."

Tom hauled Adreena to her feet. "I know exactly what she's like, I'm married to her."

"You're what?" she asked in disbelief, as Dave dragged her towards the police car hidden in the lane.

"Didn't I tell you I was married to a policeman?" shouted Hayley. "Oh, and dear Adreena, this is going to hurt you a lot more than it hurts me."

Tom held her tight. "Hayley, you're never doing anything like that again. Promise me."

"I didn't think she'd be armed. And you know I believe God gave me this gift for a reason, so that I can help others. Listen, Tom, Betty said this once. Well, she said something totally different but it struck a chord. She said, 'A ship is safe in a harbour, but that's not what a ship is for'."

"I think Betty is a very wise woman."

"Do you know, Tom, sometimes I think she is too."

Chapter 32

"Honestly, Betty, Suzie was marvellous," said Lillian the following morning. "I've never been more proud of her. She saved Hayley's life for sure."

Abigail said, "It all happened so quick. One moment it was all going well and then she pulled out a gun. I nearly died. Nobody has a gun round here."

"Rich people do, I guess," said Hayley. "I'm still shaking like a leaf. It's funny, Luna hasn't left my side since I got home last night." The young cat licked her hand as if to tell her, don't worry, I'll look after you, but don't make a habit of it.

"You don't think she'll get bail, do you?" asked Terry.

"Tom says no way. Not even with her top barrister. Not for murder and attempted murder. She'd be a certain flight risk with all her billions. She's denying it, of course. But I think once they look into the phone and car evidence, plus the admission, she won't stand a chance. Then there's the charge of having a concealed weapon and shooting at me. She can't plead not guilty to that. They found the bullet thanks to Suzie. It was in the wood, about six inches above where my head was."

Abigail said, "Next time we blackmail a heartless killer, we'll have to be more careful. What shocked me was when she admitted to killing her mother as well."

"Nobody knew how evil she was. Including me," said Hayley. "She was such a psychopath that she could hide it, because she never felt any guilt or showed any signs that she had done something so horrific. We thought Moira was bad enough, but I think Adreena Van Derson will go down in history as one of England's worst murderers."

"I don't suppose she'll pay us for the hours we did now, will she?" said Betty.

"I don't think so, hun. Sorry, Suzie. It would have been a good amount for Jordan."

"Don't worry. He's got a few more years before he goes to university. There'll be other cases. And don't forget we might get some money if we find Bertie for Mrs Plunkett."

"I nearly forgot about poor old Bertie," said Terry. "But that's an easy case. Betty and I have already solved that. We just need to tell Mrs King that Kylie Quinn is making a bit of money on the side taking on private clients. Tell Suzie about that little dog, Betty."

"It was the most adorable Cavalier King Charles Spaniel, Suzie. So cute. I know they cost a fortune, and the owners would go mad if they knew it was being kept in a shed."

"Can we go and see it, please?" begged Suzie.

"I don't think it will be there now. She was taking it back that day. She told the person on the phone that she would bring it as the owners had agreed and were bringing the money. Sorry, darling. There's lots of other ones there, but that was a sweet little thing. Poor Mrs King, she won't be pleased when you tell her, Hayley."

"I'm not looking forward to ringing her, hun."

"Then you shouldn't," said Abigail thoughtfully. "Don't ring Mrs King, Hayley. I'm sorry, but you've got to ring the police."

"It's hardly a major crime. Let the poor girl off. She's going to lose her job as it is," said Terry.

"So she should. But how else are we going to know who the accomplice is? Actually you should ring Tom straight away."

"See," said Terry. "This is why you really get on people's nerves."

"What did I do? I'm just saying what I think."

"It's the way you say things. Like you know better than us."

"Not at all. Although,…"

"See what I mean?"

"Although, I could be wrong," said Abigail, rather hurt that Terry was having a go at her again. She thought they had got past that.

Terry loved her, but he didn't always like her. Mind you, it wasn't her fault that she was opinionated and worst of all - always right. He was angry at her for knowing, and at himself, for not knowing. "Okay then, clever dick, what do you think? And I'm sorry."

"So you should be. It's just that my memory is pretty good; not that I like to blow my own trumpet." Which got a few smiles. "No, I don't. It's just that I remember that day in the library when we were looking in the Chiltern Weekly for anything about the death of Leo. And there were various articles and one was about a spate of missing pets. I know before there had been a story about gangs taking cats and dogs for ransom."

"I've heard of that too," said Betty.

"Think of what Kylie said," Abigail explained. "She said she would bring the dog and get the money. That's not how kennels work."

Betty made a fist. "How cruel. I'd throw away the key. That should have the same penalties as kidnapping a person. That poor little dog snatched away from home, and its owner not knowing what happened to it until they got a note or a phone call."

The Deadly Regatta

Hayley said, "That's another good point, Betty. That woman would know exactly the best dogs to target. She'd have all the addresses and phone numbers, and she would know exactly who would be more likely to pay up, and not call the police if the poor animal was threatened with death."

"She couldn't be seen, so I bet a friend grabbed the dogs and took them to the kennels and she kept them there till they paid up. Maybe they sold them if they refused to pay. What do you think, Terry? Do you think that's what happened?"

"Maybe," he said begrudgingly. "Yes, I reckon you're right. I'm sorry. It's just that you're so annoying."

She put her hand over her ears. "Lalala. I didn't hear the last bit. I just heard you say I'm right and you're sorry. You're forgiven, Terry. I'm sure once they've checked all the dogs at the kennels, they'll find one or two who shouldn't be there. And then they can check her friends and calls and get the person that actually steals them. I have a feeling that Bertie will be back home and growling and peeing on the floor by tomorrow."

"Another mystery solved. I think The Deadly Detective Agency is marvellous," said Betty.

"I've had another request as well from a Kerry Brooks, but I told her in an email it will be a day or so before we can get back to her. I need to clear my mind. She says her four-year-old son, Dylan, is having problems."

"What kind of problems can a four-year-old have?"

"Paranormal ones," Hayley told them. "So another little job. I feel I can't concentrate on anything until I find out why I'm still seeing that old knitted rabbit in my mind's eye."

"Maybe it belongs to the little boy, Dylan. Perhaps it's possessed or something," said Betty.

"That is a possibility. It's something important. I just wish I knew what."

Back at home the following night, Hayley was still thinking about her lingering vision. "Tom, I've got something really strange to ask you."

Tom turned over in bed to face his wife. "Even more strange than when you ask me to raid a kennel because five ghosts had told you that a kidnapping ring was being run from there?"

"Well, yes, even stranger than that."

"Go on then. But I can't think it would be more weird than that."

"Have you seen anyone lately, man or woman, with big ears, very long legs and wearing an orange striped waistcoat and orange trousers?"

"Er, no, I can't say I have. Have you?"

"Many times unfortunately. Will you tell me if you do?"

"Of course. I'm not very hopeful though. Even if I do, I can only arrest them for violations against fashion by the sound of it."

"Tell me about it. I told you it was strange. Forget it, anyway. Probably just me being daft. Do you think you'll be able to find the partner in the dog business? We need to stop saying that."

"We've got the name - Jamie Grimes. Quinn soon gave him up. And she told us where Bertie was. She said they looked identical and got mixed up. Even the collars were the same. If it hadn't been for Bertie, we might never have known about it, when you think about it. But as I said, you can have the honour of finding him and taking him home. It should be you who can tell Mrs Plunkett that you've got to the bottom of the dog business," he laughed.

Hayley groaned. "You're worse than Abigail. But I knew we would get a lead on the case, after barking up the wrong tree."

"And collar the suspect."

"We couldn't let her flea. And Abigail did a great depooment."

"Oh my God, enough, Hayl."

"Okay, hun. I'll paws." Tom decided the only way to stop her was to kiss her and pull the covers over their heads.

Chapter 33

FOR THE FIRST TIME IN MONTHS, HAYLEY WORE A warm winter coat. She turned left out of Church Lane and walked up the Becklesfield High Street to the library. Mrs Merry was putting her flowers outside her florist's and remarked about the change in weather. Mrs Hobbs and Shirley Dawkins also commented on the chill in the air as they passed her outside the Post Office. By the time she had reached the library, three more villagers had remarked about the British weather.

Inside, Janine, the librarian, bid Hayley good morning as she pushed the trolley and placed the returned books on the shelves.

Betty rushed to meet her and talked non-stop until they sat with Terry and Abigail at the far end of the library. Luckily the seats around them were empty. Hayley had picked up a random book to be reading, just in case.

"No Lillian or Suzie today?"

Abigail said, "They've gone to check on Jordan at school again. But he seems to be getting on fine since they've stopped that bully boy. And he's getting on much better with his mum now they have started talking about Suzie. And don't forget they've got to find out if that Anya is alright. Lillian thinks at the very least, she's rather neglected. But they need to see if there's anything else before you mention it to Sonia. Obviously, they don't want to tell a social worker before they know there's anything to worry about. Being poor isn't a crime and they don't want to make it worse. But Lillian and Suzie think she's hiding something from her new best friend, Camille. So we might have to investigate that at some point in the future."

"Tell them I'll do whatever I can to help, hun. Did you see the news last night? No, I don't suppose you did. It was DCI Johnson saying how his men had carried out a sting operation and got evidence to charge Adreena Van Derson on the patricide of the billionaire, Karl Van Derson. He's taking all the credit. Honestly, I nearly threw something through the screen."

Betty said, "So he not only jumped on the bandwagon, he blew his own cornet."

"I couldn't have put it better myself, hun. He made out it was all his idea to open the old man's case, and how he treats the rich and the poor all the same."

Abigail said, "Well, that bit's true. Any more news about Moira or anyone?"

"Moira is where she belongs, in jail, waiting for her trial. It will probably be next year. Same with Adreena, but I bet she'll find it harder. Rupert is putting his boat up for sale and his wife is divorcing him and going on a cruise. The funny thing is, she was one of David MacIntosh's women. And this is the amazing bit; she was the one that was paying David's rent on the fancy flat in Gorebridge. Lady Caroline told me that Ruth is selling her house in Edenbury Heights and is moving back to the stables with her mother. She'll need some help with the baby."

"I'm so pleased for her," said Betty. "Do you know if it's a girl or a boy, Hayley? I expect she'd want a girl."

"I have the feeling that she's not worried as long as everything is okay. But I think she will have a little girl again. Let's hope she is not brought up in the shadow of Patricia Rose. A child can never be as perfect as the one that has died young. Ruth needs to move on. I'm sure she will now."

"Did you ever get back to that other lady that got in touch, Hayley?"

"I did and it's very interesting. Her name is Kerry Brooks and she lives in a small village in Bedfordshire. They bought an old house that had been converted from a chapel many years ago, and they moved in when their little boy, Dylan, was born. He's four now and the trouble only started a few weeks ago. Kerry says she's too scared to live there."

"Don't tell me, it's a ghost," said Abigail.

"Nope. Three ghosts, hun. In the daytime, she often sees Dylan play with an imaginary friend. Which was okay until she saw him kick the ball to it in the garden, and the ball was kicked back again. There was nothing that it had bounced off and didn't move for a couple of seconds. And that went on for quite a while."

"That would be creepy. Especially in an old chapel," said Abigail.

"But that one seemed friendly. Kerry and her husband often felt the temperature drop when Dylan said he was playing with this other child. But now things have got worse. Especially at night and it's making him so lethargic and Kerry said he's losing weight. Dylan says there is an old lady in his room, wrapped in a shawl, who is sitting on a rocking chair that they've had since he was born. Kerry has seen it moving herself."

"Do you know, when I was alive and I saw a horror film, the two ghosts that scared me the most were old women and little children that floated about," shivered Abigail.

"Dracula films did it for me. To the day I died, I couldn't sleep if the covers weren't covering my neck," said Betty.

"Well, even that didn't worry Dylan too badly. He's obviously a brave little thing. However, another ghost has started visiting him at night time. It's this one that makes him scream, and run and get in bed with his parents. He says it's a huge man, dressed in black and he's got scary hollow eyes and lays his hand on him while he's sleeping. His mum wants to know if she should get an exorcist or if that will make it worse. I said I'd look into it and get back to her tomorrow."

"Are you going over there? It would be like one of those ghost-hunts you were telling me about, Abigail."

"Exactly. You could go with a camera and get film of it. I could help," said Abigail.

"But the family will be there and I couldn't work while they are, but you three could."

Abigail leant forward. "That is a far better idea. We could go there tonight and see exactly who these three are and if they mean Dylan any harm."

"Hmm. An old chapel, a scary old woman and a huge ghost dressed in black. I've just remembered I've got to wash my hair tonight," said Betty. "And two's company, three is not apparently."

Hayley said, "A crowd."

"Clown or not, I'm not going."

"Aw, Betty, I do love you," said Abigail. "Of course you don't have to go. Terry and I have faced worse, I think."

"I'll drop you two off tonight in Bedfordshire and you can make your own way back in the morning."

"I used to say that to my children and grandchildren every night when I put them to bed - Up the wooden hill to Bedfordshire."

"My mum used to say that too. I never knew what it meant for years," said Abigail.

Hayley was suddenly serious. "Now promise me you will both be careful. That tall shadow man could be capable of doing anything."

"Like what?" Abigail wanted to know.

"I'm not sure, but he might be able to drag you off somewhere. To hell even. And don't forget, where there's a chapel, there's likely to be graves at some time in the past."

"Er, thinking about it, Hayley, maybe the mother is right. She should get an exorcist. And my hair could do with a bit of a wash, thinking about it."

"Abigail, I'm surprised at you," said Terry. "We can't just pick and choose the easy jobs."

"Why not? Oh, okay. You know my motto - others not self."

"Really?" said Hayley, Terry and Betty together.

"Yes, really," she said, while blinking fast. "Of course I'll go. For that little boy, that's the only reason. Seriously, Terry, couldn't you take me somewhere nice next time?"

"I promise, Abi. Saturday night, you me, at the pictures."

"Good, but nothing scary for goodness sake."

Hayley dropped off Terry and Abigail at the old chapel in Criggley Cross, Bedfordshire as the sun went down. The apex roof ran from front to back on the narrow, grey brick building. The door was still housed in a gothic archway, and a stained glass window was on either side of it. Neither of these things made it welcoming for the pair of them.

Terry held Abigail's hand and smiled. "This could have been us, you know. Buying a house after we were married. Not this one, obviously. Would you have wanted me to carry you over the threshold?"

"Of course. How many children would we have had?"

"I grew up with a lot of kids in the orphanage, so I reckon about six."

"Six? I don't think so, Terry. I've got my figure to think of. And I'd really feel for you being up half the night feeding them. And think of all those nappies you'd have to change."

"Nice try, Abigail. Okay, four then."

"Two. Mum used to say that's one for each hand."

"Two for you and two for me then," said Terry.

"Okay, four. But that's my final offer. We better go and see if we can help their little boy. It'll be good practice for us."

Inside was just as dark and oppressive, with all the exposed oak beams and wood-panelling.

They could hear voices and went into the kitchen that was much lighter, as it looked like it had been added on. Mr and Mrs Brooks were tidying up after their dinner.

"Let's go and find Dylan, Terry. He must be in bed by now."

They went up the wooden stairs and saw an open door, with a lamp shining through the gap.

"This must be it, Abigail. Now stand behind me and do exactly as I say." Not that she ever had before, he thought.

They crept in, checking carefully behind the door. A small boy was sitting on the floor playing with a small train set. He looked up quickly when he saw them and jumped to his feet.

"It's alright, Dylan. Don't be scared, we're here to help you." The boy pointed to the bed, where another small boy was sleeping soundly, with one leg out of the covers. "I'm sorry, sweetheart, you must be Dylan's friend. Aren't you adorable? Can you tell us your name?"

A voice from the corner of the room made them shriek. Rocking on her chair was the old woman. "He don't talk. Never has, never will. He's called William. What ya doing here?"

"We're only here to help. I'm Abigail and this is Terry. The boy's mother is worried about him, so she contacted a friend of ours."

"She's right to be worried."

"Because of the man that comes? Is he an evil spirit or demon?"

That made the old lady cackle. "Nah. Who told you that? He's a right good man. If it wasn't for him, we wouldn't know."

"Know what?" asked Abigail.

"Know yon little 'un is dying." A dark shadow blew in

through the window. "That's good timing. This here is Jeremiah Pickett. Doctor Jeremiah Pickett."

Abigail sighed with relief. She wouldn't have to fight for her soul. "Nice to meet you, Doctor. We're only here because you've been frightening the boy. His parents have been scared stiff."

"I didn't mean to scare anyone, but you can feel so helpless sometimes."

"We know all about that, sir. That's why we want to help," said Terry. "Can you tell us what's going on?"

"Apart from young William here, we've kept our distance. But we've watched. There's not much else to do, is there? And over the months, I've seen him playing in the garden, then getting out of breath. He's had to sit down and he looks tired and pale. Since then I've seen how his feet and ankles look swollen and there's a bluish colour around the lips. I know enough about hearts to know there's something radically wrong with his. I can feel the irregular beat and it's not right. I'm telling you, he could die before the week is out."

Terry and Abigail looked at each other. They almost felt like it was one of their children that was in trouble. Abigail walked over to the bed to look at the angelic little boy and stroked his hair. "Don't worry, Dylan, you're going to be fine, sweetheart. We're not going to let you die."

Chapter 34

"That poor little boy. It nearly broke my heart, but he's going to be fine," Hayley told the others. "Kerry literally picked him up from his nursery and took him straight to the hospital after I told her. Turns out he had an undetected heart defect. That doctor was right. They kept him in, there and then, and are going to operate tomorrow. Thank the Lord, he's going to be okay. I feel it in my bones."

"Well done, Hayley. You did a really good thing," said Lillian. "I worked in the children's ward for years and I know exactly what those poor parents would have gone through. He could have survived the heart attack, but they don't always."

"And starting school, he would have been playing in the playground and it could have happened at any time. I did ask, but Dylan hasn't ever had a rabbit, knitted or otherwise, unfortunately. So, after I told Kerry and she left, I looked for the three spirits and found them in the garden. I asked what I could do for them, and it turned out they all needed help to cross over, bless them. The doctor had a wife to meet, the old woman had five children she wanted to see again, and I cried my eyes out when this happened. The little boy, William, who they told me hadn't spoken a word for fifty years, raised his arms and said 'Mama' and ran towards the light. I don't think I've ever felt so emotional."

Betty put her hands on her cheeks. "Oh, bless him. Don't start me off, please. That is so sad." Suzie went over and gave her a hug.

"Even I'm crying," said Abigail. "He was so cute. We would have loved a little boy like him, wouldn't we, Terry? Actually, we could have adopted him in a way. We could have brought him here if he had wanted." Terry squeezed her hand and for the first time, gave her a kiss in front of the others.

"That's a wonderful thought, Abi. I worry enough about Luna. I'm not sure I could stand the worry of a child after what just happened," said Hayley.

Betty said, "That's the trouble. Children are the biggest worry you can ever have. But also the biggest joy and love. For all the heartaches, I wouldn't have missed it for the world."

Hayley said, "Maybe, one day. Now, talking of Luna, I'd better get home, because Tom isn't there to feed him. He's gone to see his parents and give them a hand. They're having a clear-out and downsizing to a smaller house. He says I've got to check it out before they buy one, just in case it's haunted. He would never have said that a year ago. He's a true believer now."

"Do you want us to come with you when you check it out?" asked Abigail, hoping she would.

"Not with, but a trip after dark might be a good idea. These things come at night, mostly," she said with a smile. "So we'll meet up tomorrow. You never know, there might be a client, living or dead, that gets in touch tonight."

After feeding Luna and giving him his cuddles until he was bored, Hayley lit a candle and lay down in the conservatory. The music she played soon helped her to drift off into a dreamless sleep. The kind she liked best. All too soon, she heard Tom shouting out that he was home.

"Hayley!"

"In the conservatory, hun," she said as she struggled up.

"Look what Mum gave me. She found it in the attic."

Hayley sat down again. It was a white rabbit, with long legs and dressed in orange.

"His name's Hatty. I used to love him when I was young. I'd forgotten all about it. My nan knitted it for me. Mum said she kept it for when I have a kid. Apparently, it was my favourite teddy when I felt poorly. She says she can't wait to be a grandma. What do you think, Hayl? It made me really think about it."

"A baby? I thought we'd agreed Luna was enough to handle."

"I know. But if we can love a kitten, imagine how much we would love our own little boy."

"Or girl. I'm not sure, hun. The last few weeks haven't been that good an advert for having kids. One child was killed in a car crash, one nearly died of a heart attack, and one killed her mum and dad."

"But apart from that," joked Tom.

"It would be nice, I suppose. I hear about Betty's love for her family and Suzie's for Sonia, so it can't be that bad. It's funny how it's all linked together with the cases. Coincidence or fate? One of life's signs, for sure. I'll think about it, I promise, Tom."

"I love you, Hayley. Imagine our own little boy running around the place."

"Or little girl. We could start now if you like," said Hayley seductively.

"Okay. I better get this though," he said as the phone rang. Hayley sat down, knowing he had been called into work. "Sorry, darling, I've got to go. There's been another murder. You better go and fetch the others, this sounds a really odd one. Here you are, take Hatty and think it over. How funny, he's dressed in an orange waistcoat and trousers like you were on about. What are the chances of that? I'll phone you as soon as I can." Tom gave her a quick kiss and went.

Hayley lay back down. There was no rush to go and see the others, and she was still thinking about having a baby. She looked at Hatty, realising what someone had been trying to tell her. She was in no hurry though. She was enjoying the work with the agency too much. But if it did happen, she would have to get Betty to teach her to knit. Maybe she could go to the haberdashers in the High Street tomorrow and buy a pair of needles and some wool. "Pink? No, Tom was right, blue."

One thing was certain, her little boy would have a lot of aunties and a wonderful uncle from the other side. And he would always be protected by Suzie all his life.

Still, that was in the future. Right now she had better get all the gang together for this latest murder. Tom would soon be ringing with all the details, and they would need to get there fast. Hayley got up and sat Hatty in her place.

She had a vision and had to smile to herself. Oh dear, Tom would absolutely hate it, but she had no doubt that the two children they were going to have would both be as psychic and gifted as their mother!!

THE END

Acknowledgments

A special thank you to Miika Hannila at Next Chapter for publishing my book, and to Petteri Hannila for the excellent layout.

Also, many thanks to Lordan June Pinote, who has done another excellent cover.

About the Author

Ann Parker was born in Hertfordshire, England and still lives there with her husband, Terry, and her black and white cat, Jazz.

She is the author of the Abigail Summers Cozy Mysteries - The Deadly Detective Agency, The Deadly Pub Quiz & The Deadly Regatta, and the short story book entitled Magic & Memories.

Ann has had poems published on Spillwords and in the best-selling anthologies, Hidden in Childhood and Petals of Haiku, as well as various magazines.

When she is not writing, she loves to spend time with her family or reading a good whodunit.

To learn more about Ann Parker and discover more Next Chapter authors, visit our website at www.nextchapter.pub.

Printed in Dunstable, United Kingdom